BLOODLINE

BOOK TWO

RECKONING

Also by Kate Cary

Bloodline

BLOODLINE

BOOK TWO

RECKONING

A NOVEL BY
KATE CARY

razOr
bill

Bloodline Book Two: Reckoning

RAZORBILL

Published by the Penguin Group
Penguin Young Readers Group
345 Hudson Street, New York, New York 10014, U.S.A.
Penguin Group (USA) Inc., 375 Hudson Street, New York, New York 10014, U.S.A.
Penguin Group (Canada), 90 Eglinton Avenue East, Suite 700, Toronto,
Ontario, Canada M4P 2Y3 (a division of Pearson Penguin Canada Inc.)
Penguin Books Ltd, 80 Strand, London WC2R 0RL, England
Penguin Ireland, 25 St Stephen's Green, Dublin 2, Ireland
(a division of Penguin Books Ltd)
Penguin Group (Australia), 250 Camberwell Road, Camberwell,
Victoria 3124, Australia (a division of Pearson Australia Group Pty Ltd)
Penguin Books India Pvt Ltd, 11 Community Centre, Panchsheel Park,
New Delhi – 110 017, India
Penguin Group (NZ), 67 Apollo Drive, Rosedale, North Shore 0632,
New Zealand (a division of Pearson New Zealand Ltd.)
Penguin Books (South Africa) (Pty) Ltd, 24 Sturdee Avenue, Rosebank,
Johannesburg 2196, South Africa

Penguin Books Ltd, Registered Offices: 80 Strand, London WC2R 0RL, England

10 9 8 7 6 5 4 3 2 1

LIBRARY OF CONGRESS HAS CATALOGED THE HARDCOVER EDITION AS FOLLOWS:

Cary, Kate.
  Bloodline : reckoning / by Kate Cary.
    p. cm. — (Bloodline ; bk. 2)
  Summary: In this story told primarily through journal entries, Quincey Harker, the heir
to Dracula's bloodline, returns to England in 1918 to pursue Nurse Mary Seward, whose
fiance has been transformed into a monstrous vampire.
  ISBN 978-1-59514-013-5
  [1. Vampires—Fiction. 2. Diaries—Fiction. 3. Horror stories.] I. Title. II. Title:
Reckoning.
  PZ7.C2629Bp 2007
  [Fic]—dc22
                                                          2006101841

Razorbill paperback ISBN: 978-1-59514-179-8

Printed in the United States of America

For Matt Haslum

Prayer to Saint Michael the Archangel

Holy Michael Archangel, defend us in the day of battle.

Be our safeguard against the wickedness and snares of the devil.

May God rebuke him, we humbly pray.

And do, thou Prince of the Heavenly Host, thrust down to hell Satan, and all the other wicked spirits who wander through the world for the ruin of souls. . . .

Amen.

PROLOGUE

Clyst Abbey, Devon
Daybook of
Father Michael, Abbot of Clyst

13TH NOVEMBER 1917

3:05 A.M.

Thanks be to God that we have made it through another night.

My sleep has been fitful, disturbed again by the unearthly noises coming from the prisoner's cell. Lord have mercy on us all if he should break loose while the bloodlust is upon him. Though I know that his chains are strong and the lock on his cell door heavy, fear clutches my throat when I am caught in his fiery gaze.

When the moon is at its highest, his tortured groans echo down the stone hallways—normally so still with the silence kept by our Cistercian brotherhood—until the whole abbey seems to ring with his torment.

He howls for blood, of course—craving it to nourish the darkness within him. Our keeping him from it strikes hard at his blackened heart.

As I write, he howls still—but less fiercely now, with dawn coming. The daylight shall quieten his vampire soul.

By starving him—chaining him so that he cannot indulge his bloodlust—I pray we might eventually cause the evil that possesses him to shrivel and die.

Shall the mortal remains of Quincey Harker survive such trial?

That I do not know. I have come across no record of such exorcism being embarked upon before.

I must hasten to the chapel. Prayers will begin soon. The early morning vigil calms me now more than it has ever done—warm candlelight flickering on the smooth stone pillars, white robes swishing against the gleaming wood of the pews as the brothers lower themselves to kneel alongside me to pray.

Afterward will come the blessed light of dawn. And Harker will be still again. . . .

11:05 P.M.

I fear that sleep is proving impossible tonight. The presence of our prisoner, locked below, has truly unsettled our community.

As I entered the refectory for supper this evening, the room hummed with whispering. The brothers, seated at the rows of long wooden tables, glanced up, eyeing me anxiously before returning to their hushed conversations.

"Good evening, brothers," I said. "Is all well with you?"

Brother Sebastian glanced uneasily across at Brother Stephen but ventured nothing.

I took my place at table, said grace, and then helped myself to stew and bread, the latter freshly made that morning in the abbey's bakery.

And then Brother Sebastian began to speak. "Father, how can we be well when we harbor evil beneath our roof?" he asked quietly.

"Harker was more unsettled than ever last night," Brother Stephen added. He gazed at me, his blue eyes earnest in his gaunt face. "He seems to be making no improvement."

I understood their concerns. Even I, in the darkest hours before dawn, have questioned whether we really have any hope of redeeming Quincey Harker's twisted soul. But there must always be hope. "I beseech you, brothers, keep your faith. We must not abandon this work," I insisted. "With no fresh blood to sustain it, the evil in Harker must surely be weakening."

"That may be, but his will remains fearsome," whispered Brother Sebastian.

"Maybe we should take a leaf from the old lunatic asylums," grunted Brother Matthew, breaking a hunk of bread with his rough, stout fingers. "They'd 'ave beaten the devil out of Quincey Harker. Flogged 'im and purged 'im with emetics." He pushed a piece of the bread into his mouth and began to chew.

I shook my head. "Brother Matthew, this is 1917, and we are men of God. I hope we have left such barbarism behind."

"We may have," Brother Stephen said. "But Quincey Harker hasn't!"

I stared at him, surprised at the harshness of his tone. His voice dropped to a whisper. "Harker is a vampire!" he insisted. "There is no saving him. His soul is irredeemably lost. Surely it would be safer for all if he were destroyed in the traditional way."

"A stake through the heart!" I exclaimed. "Brother, we are not murderers!"

All but Brother Stephen looked away. "It would not be murder," he argued. "We would be freeing his soul at last and ridding the world of a great evil."

"Brother Stephen." I sighed. "Do you have so little faith in prayer? And what of God's mercy? Our Lord Jesus spoke of love—it is the most powerful weapon. We can weaken the evil that grips Harker's soul by depriving it of the blood it craves. And once it is weakened, we must trust that God will show mercy and cleanse the darkness from him once and for all. Remember the words of Saint Paul: God's strength manifests itself when I am weak.

Now Brother Stephen looked away too.

"We must believe that God's love has the power to save Quincey Harker," I went on. "And we must be his vessels."

As I write, moonlight flooding my desk, brighter than the candle flickering beside the page, I can hear Harker begin his own midnight vigil—the mournful, agonized howls piercing the thick stone walls to ring out into the night.

I pray tonight that my words prove true and that we can indeed save Quincey Harker's immortal soul.

29TH NOVEMBER 1917

After prayers and breaking fast this morning, I visited Harker in his cell.

I entered the dank, stone chamber, closing its iron door behind me. The heaviness of the earthy-smelling air made it hard to breathe.

Harker was resting in the shadiest corner, away from the weak shaft of sunlight filtering through the tiny barred window high up on one of the walls. He was sitting on the floor, his head leaning wearily against the stones. But his eyes glinted watchfully. He reminded me of a caged panther I had once seen at London Zoo.

"You should sleep," I advised. "You must be tired."

"I have no wish to sleep," he growled, staring in disgust at his narrow, blanketed bunk.

"But is it not in the nature of your kind to sleep through the day?" I asked.

Harker sprang to his feet, the heavy chains that bound his wrists clanking in protest. "I may hide from the flesh-burning sun, but I am not such a slave to the vampire nature as most of my kind. I am a *prince* among them," he hissed, his eyes flashing. "My power is far greater than any of theirs."

I took a stumbling step back, a hand sliding to my crucifix. His sudden anger alarmed me. Even though it was daytime, I feared I might glimpse that fiery glow that rages in his eyes when the hunger for prey grips him.

His gaze retained its dark intensity, however. Harker pushed a lock of black hair away from his forehead and then, to my surprise, he smiled. "It is you who should get some sleep," he warned. "For tonight is Saint Andrew's Eve—when all the world's evils are at their strongest." He drew in a long breath. "My hunger is sure to be . . . most disturbing."

I fought the icy fear that chilled my blood at his words, thinking instead of his howls of anguish ringing out each night. "I'm sorry your hunger torments you so," I told him. "But we keep you here in your best interests. And tonight we shall pray for you."

Harker lifted his chin and let out a harsh laugh. "Do you believe God will listen?"

"God is always listening," I assured him.

"But does he always *hear*?" Harker asked.

I returned his gaze uncertainly. Was he taunting me?

"I pray that someday you will know his mercy," I murmured, and stepped toward the heavy iron door.

As I turned the key in the lock from the other side of it, I saw Harker still watching me through its small barred window. I looked away.

What am I to make of our prisoner? After listening to him curse and struggle against his captivity each night, I hardly expected to find his conversation still so lucid. But can I believe it is Harker with whom I speak? Am I conversing with a man or with the evil that possesses him? I pray that the Lord in His infinite wisdom will give us the strength to bring this tormented soul back into the light.

The moon is rising—and, I fear, a storm is too. The dark crags and rolling heath land beyond the abbey walls are now brushed by glowering skies. Though the seasons here in the West Country are known for their mildness, Dartmoor seems to have a climate of its own—as if the moor itself draws down the worst of the elements and conjures up squalls and tempests like some ancient stormbringer. On nights like this, staring out into that bleak landscape beyond, one feels very far from civilization. It is hard to believe that the busy cathedral city of Exeter is but a few miles away.

I shall now join the brothers for a night of prayer. For on tonight of all nights, we must do all that we can to protect Harker from the evil within him.

30TH NOVEMBER 1917

I must record the horrors I have just seen.

Last night, as I led the brothers in prayer for Harker, terrible groans of torment began to rise from his cell below. And then, just before midnight, a scream rang out from the cell— a scream so chilling that it seemed to choke me into silence.

I picked up an altar candle and, signaling Brother Sebastian to do the same and follow me, hurried down toward the vaults.

Harker's cell door stood ajar.

Brother Sebastian looked at me, his customarily ruddy cheeks stricken white with terror.

The most monstrous howling could not have filled me with more trepidation than the heavy silence that came from within the cell. Had Harker somehow escaped? And was he now at large?

I prayed for strength to stop my hand from shaking as I reached out and pushed the door open wider.

Harker was there. His chains still hung upon his wrists,
shackling him to the wall. But he seemed insensible to our arrival, for his attention was entirely focused on the white-robed figure slumped in his strong grasp. For moments I could neither move nor speak, watching him convulse in rhythmic shudders as he sucked the lifeblood from his vic-tim's throat, thick groans of gratification rumbling up from his own. And then, in one swift movement, Harker twisted his prey's neck and I heard the cracking of bone.

The victim's head lolled back unnaturally, neck clearly broken. His face was contorted like that of a gargoyle, the dead whites of his eyes like marble in the cold moonlight that sliced through the tiny barred window above.

It was Brother Stephen.

I found my voice. "No!" My cry echoed around the cell.

Harker raised his head, his lips and chin gleaming wet with blood. His eyes glowed like embers as he met my stricken gaze. He let Brother Stephen fall to the cold flag-stones. Blood oozed from Brother Stephen's throat like that of a slaughtered lamb, staining the white wool of his robe.

I sank to my knees beside Brother Stephen's body. "Why did you come here, Brother?" I sobbed, though I knew he could no longer hear me.

And then I saw them: the mallet and long, sharpened wooden stake, lying in the corner of the cell as though flung there. Brother Stephen had decided to take matters into his own hands. He had come here to kill Harker—to hammer a stake through his evil heart. God rest his poor, impetuous soul.

"Father Michael, come away!" Brother Sebastian had followed me in and was pulling at my robe. "The prisoner is still possessed! You must come out of his reach!"

But God must have entered my soul like iron, for I felt no fear within me as I looked up and met Harker's fiery stare. Only sorrow.

I lifted my crucifix and, holding it out in front of me, walked slowly toward Harker. "Know that the Lord sees what you have done and abhors it!" I proclaimed.

He roared at the sight of the blessed object and tugged at his chains, his face frenzied. A superhuman strength seemed to possess him. With an almighty heave, he wrenched the iron wristbands and snapped them from the chains that held him. The chains clattered against the wall, dangling useless now from their fastenings. He was free!

Harker lunged forward, pushing me out of his way. My fall was broken by the still-warm body of Brother Stephen. Drawing in a sharp breath, I turned to see Harker charge past a cowering Brother Sebastian and through the open cell door.

"We must stop him," I gasped as Brother Sebastian helped me to my feet.

"Father Michael, I fear he is unstoppable . . ." Brother Sebastian whispered.

"Then we must return to the brothers in the chapel and pray for Brother Stephen's safe passage to heaven—and for any poor souls caught out on the fog-wrapped moors. For now, no creature is safe. Having hungered for blood for so long, I dare not imagine how much it will take to slake Harker's thirst."

Dawn is now lighting the sky. I have returned to my cell to rest after our vigils, but I cannot sleep. Some of the brothers are still praying. It is a mercy, at least, that Brother Stephen died of a broken neck and not from being sucked dry of his blood. His body will not rise as one of the vampire undead. It is the one mercy Harker showed his poor victim.

Despite his crimes, we pray for Quincey Harker too. What could have made such a monster, and who can save his blackened soul now?

CHAPTER 1

Journal of
Quincey Harker

OXFORD UNIVERSITY*
31ST OCTOBER 1908

What a charmed life I have led here at Oxford—not least for the mortal pleasures I have encountered. The appeal of warm, yielding flesh is undeniable—as is the thrill of seduction. But having witnessed the more craven pleasures enjoyed by the initiated at Castle Dracula last summer . . . knowing what is to come . . . I fear that university life may now feel rather tame.

I long for my own initiation—to feel the primal power that I'm told lies dormant in my blood. My body and soul will then awaken to their full vampiric glory, and I shall take my place, alongside Father, as a prince among my kind. A descendant of Dracula himself.

Before I left Transylvania, I asked again when my initiation would be, but Father only repeated that it would come when I was ready. Surely it must be soon! Watching is no longer enough. I want to enjoy the full privileges of my birthright.

Meanwhile I must concern myself with trivialities, like the letter that arrived from Father this morning. He has asked me to greet a distant cousin of mine who is arriving in Oxford for a few days next week to do research at the Bodleian Library. I have never heard of her—she has not attended any of the Saint Andrew's Eve festivities at the castle—and I wonder if she is even one of us. But Father asked me to be polite and show her the sights, so I suppose I'd better.

I only hope she does not turn out to be one of those hearty, boring bluestocking types.

5TH NOVEMBER 1908

Rebecca is certainly no bluestocking. . . .

When the train arrived at midnight, the auburn-haired beauty who alighted took my breath away.

She turned to look at me. "Quincey Harker?" she asked, her voice rich and melodic.

I nodded, feeling foolishly shy, and could not help but stare as the movement of air from the departing train caused her fur coat to billow open and expose the silk-covered curve of her hips.

"Quincey . . . How wonderful to meet you at last." She smiled, holding a slender gloved hand out to me.

"The pleasure is mine," I answered a little hoarsely, taking her hand in my own. I could see she was well assured of her own allure and knew how she stirred me.

"I suppose you know nothing about me," she said with a teasing smile as she handed me her case.

"No," I replied apologetically.

"Oh, don't worry," she said. "There is plenty of time for us to get to know each other. . . ." She looked around the station. "Now, where are you taking me?"

I was somewhat put off my stride, being used to dominating most social situations. "I—I booked you into the Randolph Hotel," I stammered. "I thought we'd take a taxi there."

"Oh, must we?" she said. "I much prefer to walk. I find the night air so refreshing." She inhaled deeply and then, giving a contented sigh, turned toward the exit.

I heard the silk of her stockings swish as she moved. "We can walk if you like—it's not far," I said.

"Oh, good." She smiled and handed me her other bag.

My small talk as we made our way to the hotel was, I'm sure, rather inane. I could not take my eyes off her. Though I tried my best to be charming, I was relieved when we reached our destination.

"Thank you, Quincey," she said as we made our way into

the foyer. "I presume you've made a reservation in my name?"

I nodded and then informed reception of her arrival. The bellboy hurried over to collect Rebecca's luggage and show her to her room.

She turned to me with a languid smile. "Come up with me," she invited. "Keep me company while I settle in. I hate that desolate feeling one encounters when first entering an unfamiliar room—especially when alone."

I could tell she knew I would agree without hesitation.

After tipping the bellboy, I sat down to wait in the parlor of Rebecca's suite while she unpacked in a bedroom leading off it.

Her presence agitated me, but not unpleasurably so. . . . I felt a curious urge to be out in the night, breathing the sharp air and striding through the shadowed streets.

Rebecca came back into the parlor. My throat tightened as I saw she had changed into a silken lilac gown that betrayed every curve of her body beneath it.

I watched silently as she bent to take a cigarette from the silver box on the table, pushing away the lock of auburn hair that fell across her face. She pressed the cigarette into a long platinum holder and lit it.

I heard the whisper of her robe against the velvet upholstery as she sank down onto a plump green sofa. The soft sound thrilled me.

"Your father tells me you're a bright young man," she commented, looking up at me. She patted the empty space next to her.

Heart pounding, I walked slowly across the room and sat next to her. She smelled exquisite. "I suppose I am," I answered. "The work here isn't difficult. I'm told I shall graduate with honors next summer. Do you know my father well?"

"Not very well," Rebecca replied, "but he was eager we should meet while we were both in England."

"Oh?" I was intrigued. "Where do you usually live?"

"Nowhere for long. I tend to keep on the move." Rebecca turned and stubbed out her cigarette in the ashtray behind the sofa. Her movement revealed the smooth outline of her breasts and belly, pressing against the silk of her gown. My mouth went dry.

She turned back to see me staring at her and gave me a gratified smile. "I think we shall have fun together, Quincey Harker," she said.

Anticipation caused my heart to race, my skin to tingle. Did Rebecca plan seduction?

"But for now . . ." she added, a trace of apology in her tone, "I must rest."

Disappointment coursed through me. "Of course," I replied politely, and immediately got to my feet.

Rebecca's smooth fingers touched mine. They felt chilled,

like highly polished marble. "You'll come again tomorrow evening?" she asked. "I shall be waiting for you, Quincey. . . ."

Her tone was anything but familial. I felt my body tighten with desire. "Yes," I replied.

I saw something glint within the depths of Rebecca's cool green eyes. A fiery glow I had seen before—at the castle on Saint Andrew's Eve.

A delicious suspicion began to stir in my mind. The time of my initiation had finally arrived.

With reluctance, I broke my gaze away from hers and strode toward the door.

7TH NOVEMBER 1908

Yesterday I celebrated my twenty-first birthday and, in the depths of night, my true coming of age.

I had made my excuses to the university crowd so that I could spend the evening with Rebecca as promised. And from the way we had left things the day before, I half hoped, half expected that Rebecca would lead me straight to her bed.

To my surprise, she suggested we leave the sensual haven of her hotel room to venture out for a walk instead. Swallowing my frustration, I agreed.

We wandered, arm in arm, along the dark, cobbled

streets. The touch of her seemed to impart some dark energy, infusing my flesh, heightening its awareness.

"How quiet and empty the town seems," I breathed.

Rebecca gave a low laugh. "Appearances can be deceptive, Quincey." She tightened her grip on my arm. "Behind all those college walls are warm, slumbering bodies, softly breathing, gently pulsing with fresh, sweet blood." She gave a little shiver and licked her lips. I could sense that she was nearly as aroused as I was by her words.

I felt a thrust of overwhelming longing for her. I pulled her fiercely against me. For a few brief moments, she yielded to my embrace—and then she gently pushed me away.

"Soon . . ." she whispered. "Very soon . . ."

She took my arm and started walking once more, steering me across the street toward the entrance of the churchyard opposite. I looked at her, confused, as she led me through the gate. I felt an instinctive loathing at the sight of the church towering in the darkness above us and wondered why Rebecca had brought me here.

Silently she led me between the elms, among the graves, and eventually stopped beside a low stone plinth. She reclined upon it, curling and stretching like a cat. She began to stroke the gravestone, and I watched as her long fingers traced the name inscribed there.

"This is the grave of a murderer," she told me. "He killed his wife, yet was not condemned for it, because she had been unfaithful to him. He lived out his years unjudged by his peers, but once he died, his soul received its just reward. Come. Touch. Can you feel the suffering contained within?"

I bent to run my fingers across the mossed and weathered stone. They prickled at the feel of its surface and a new, quite thrilling sensation began to pulsate through my veins.

"Is it not delightful to find such evil lurking amid godliness?" Rebecca murmured. She closed her eyes and leaned back on the stone, her coat falling open to reveal the dove gray satin dress she wore beneath.

I cannot say what excited me most, the sight of Rebecca's satin-clad body, shining silver in the moonlight—or the energy that my body seemed to draw from the grave she lay upon.

Rebecca slid her hands under my coat and pulled me down to her. She raked her silver-lacquered nails into my back. The violent tearing against my flesh only heightened my passion. I kissed her fiercely and she responded with equal force, pressing her open mouth against mine.

And then, I felt her kisses slide away from my mouth. I shuddered in anticipation. With utter rapture, I saw her lips part to reveal two beautifully pointed white fangs. She rolled me over and leaned down over me, her long hair cascading onto my chest. I felt her mouth upon my throat— and then gasped as two needle-sharp points gripped my throat and pierced my flesh, bearing down hard, stretching the surrounding skin until I felt it might split. But I didn't care. Pleasure and pain had become one. Rebecca drank and drank, the beating of my heart and her drawing of my blood in perfect, rhythmic unison.

I felt my heart flicker . . . and then stop.

Darkness closed around me.

CHAPTER 2

Journal of
Quincey Harker

7TH NOVEMBER *(CONTINUED)*

My next awareness was of a slow, languorous awakening. I had no notion of whether seconds, minutes, or even hours had passed. I opened my eyes to see the moon still high in the sky. Rebecca was gazing down at me, her lips ruby red, glistening with my own blood.

"So . . . Quincey Harker . . ." she breathed. "It is done."

I inhaled a deep lungful of the cold night air, feeling a surge of energy that seemed to possess my very being. This time it was I who pulled Rebecca to me.

The reddish glow began to return to her beautiful eyes. "I'm so glad it was I who was chosen to awaken you," she murmured, tracing a fingernail over my chest.

A new and desperate craving pierced me. The strange fascination I had always felt for blood turned into a wild desire. "It is I who am fortunate," I told her, capturing her hand in mine to kiss its cool palm. "You have taught me well. But I have still to give my own bloody kiss . . ." I ventured softly. "Who is it that shall be first?"

Rebecca's eyes now flamed with reignited passion. "You start," she began, "with me."

I lowered my head toward her soft, exposed throat. She gave a groan of pleasure at the touch of my tongue as I traced its tip along her pearl-white flesh. I felt the pulsing within and became aware of a curious tingling sensation in my gums. There was a moment of pain. And then, against the flesh of my lower lip, I felt my incisors lengthen into razor-sharp fangs.

Heady with anticipation now, reeling with desire, I drew my lips back over the smooth new enamel—and then I pressed down, my fangs piercing Rebecca's skin like needles through satin.

The first metallic spurt of her blood gushed into my mouth. I gagged from the force of its flow but quickly gauged her heart's rhythm and began to swallow with each pulse.

The taste of it was beyond all pleasure. My tongue quivered under its bittersweet tang. Rebecca gasped ecstatically in my arms. Only when I felt her growing limp did I stop, fearful of taking more than she could give. I looked down at her face. Her eyes seemed glazed, and I feared for a moment

I had harmed her—but then she grasped my head to draw my mouth to hers and kissed away the blood that smeared my lips.

"Oh, Quincey . . ." she murmured between kisses. "I envy the mortal who receives your kiss on Saint Andrew's Eve!"

I started at her words, still immersed in what we had just shared. "I need no mortal," I whispered into her hair. "Only you."

She gazed earnestly into my eyes. "Darling. My blood, while enticing, is not enough. Only mortal blood can complete the transformation I have begun—bring you your full birthright of power."

"I shall do without it!" I exclaimed recklessly.

Eyes wide, Rebecca shook her head and laughed. "Quincey, please . . . Wait until Saint Andrew's Eve. You'll feel differently then. You are Dracula's heir! How can you not claim your birthright?"

I sighed and pulled her to me. "Saint Andrew's Eve is weeks away," I told her. "Until then, I have you. . . ."

"Of course you do, darling," she replied, running a gentle finger along my cheek.

As we walked back to her hotel to escape the fast-approaching dawn, I reveled in the euphoria Rebecca had awoken in my body, the sensation of strength that infused my heart with a wild joy.

On reaching the hotel entrance, Rebecca reached up and

lightly kissed my lips. I looked down into her face in surprise. Was I not invited in?

"It has been a momentous night, my darling," she said gently. "You need to rest—and you will do so better in your own bed." She gave a knowing little grin.

I pulled her against me and kissed her hard on the lips. "No doubt you are right," I replied. "I shall return tonight."

"Tonight . . ." she repeated. And then she disappeared into the hotel.

I made my way back here, to my lodgings, and though I shall count the hours until I am back with Rebecca, I am glad of the opportunity to record these momentous events while they are still fresh in my mind.

How did I ever think myself alive before this?

LATER

When I returned to her hotel, Rebecca was gone. I was told by the desk clerk that she'd checked out in a great hurry, just minutes after arriving back at the hotel before dawn. The clerk grew pale at the fury that must have shown on my face as I ripped open the cream envelope she had left for me. I snatched out the folded sheet of paper within and read its brief contents.

Dearest Quincey,

My task is finished. I hope you will remember what we have shared with fondness.

Your servant,

Rebecca

Damn her! And damn me, for thinking she was anything but a whore, bought and paid for by my family. I knew, of course, that she had been sent to me, that our encounter had had a purpose beyond intimacy—but I had not taken her for the heartless wench she had now proved herself to be. How dare she abandon me just minutes after what we had shared!

Fondness.

No, Rebecca. I don't feel fondness.

I feel betrayal and rage.

If I knew where you had gone, I would pursue you and drain you dry for leaving me with that cold, polite little note.

So what now? Saint Andrew's Eve cannot come too soon. As far as I am concerned, Rebecca can turn to dust. I shall throw myself into the festivities at Castle Dracula with relish and claim my birthright.

What power will I feel then, when my transformation is complete?

I have arrived home.

My body is weary after my long journey to Castle Dracula, but my mind races with anticipation of what is to come.

These past three weeks have been hard, but I have resisted my newfound craving for blood. It has always been the family's wish that I should come into my full power and birthright on Saint Andrew's Eve—the night when all evil in the world is at its most potent. And tonight that wish shall be fulfilled.

Oh, how I shall feast!

No doubt Father has already acquired suitable prey for me, but the stinging memory of Rebecca has driven me to make my own choice for this occasion.

And I have chosen well, I think: a Frenchwoman I met on the train from Paris to Munich. Her name is Collette. She is beautiful, naturally, and intent on using this to her full advantage. I can tell that she believes she has quite captivated me, the foolish little gold digger. She was delighted at the invitation to accompany me here—and was willing to give all, there and then, in our railway carriage. But I have, of course, saved her for tonight. She is in her room now, dressing for dinner.

I had thought Father and Mother might be shocked at my

bringing someone home. But if so, they hid it well when they saw me helping Collette from the carriage that brought us from the station earlier this evening.

"Quincey . . ." Father stretched out his hand to shake mine. "Rebecca tells me she enjoyed meeting you," he added immediately.

My heart lurched at the mention of her name, and so unexpectedly soon. I forced myself to give a casual shrug. "Is she here for the celebrations?" I asked.

Father shook his head. "I thought it best not." He held my gaze for a moment. "She has played her part."

I felt frustration flare in my chest and clenched my fists.

Mother's hand brushed my mine gently. "I see you have brought your own guest, Quincey! Aren't you going to introduce us?" Her eyes glittered approvingly as she cast her gaze over Collette's shapely figure.

I turned to Collette—who was glancing up at the impressive walls of the castle, her eyes sparkling with avaricious interest—and made the introductions.

"You are very welcome here, my dear," Mother crooned to my unsuspecting prey. "I hope Quincey told you tonight is a very special occasion?"

"Oh yes—some sort of anniversary, I understand. I hope I'm not imposing," Collette replied, somewhat unconvincingly.

"Of course not, my dear," Mother assured her smoothly. "We like fresh blood in the place." She took hold of

Collette's arm, smiled at me, and then led Collette into the castle. The torches around the structure, already lit, sent a red glow rippling over the cobbled courtyard as they passed through it.

Father squeezed my shoulder. "Good to have you home, Quincey. I have been looking forward to this night since the day you came into this world. I know you won't disappoint me."

"No, Father, I won't," I assured him. "Now if you will excuse me, I shall go and prepare for the celebrations."

I came up here to my room and found it little changed.

But how changed *I* am!

I can hear hooves in the courtyard. Guests are beginning to arrive. I must go down and help Father greet them.

30TH NOVEMBER 1908

It is not yet dawn, but I am exhausted. Before I allow myself to sleep, however, I am determined to record every detail of this momentous night. . . .

"What an extraordinary place!" Collette whispered as we took our places at table in the Great Hall. She looked somewhat taken aback to find herself amid such opulence and among so many other guests.

And her unease grew, of course, once the meal was over. . . .

Mother graciously led the revelers along the corridor to the drawing room. The men began to throw aside their jackets and unknot their ties; women cast off their shawls and stoles to reveal low-cut gowns, exposing their creamy flesh. Little by little, the formal facade kept up throughout dinner began to fall away. Couples and threesomes sprawled upon the furniture in the most relaxed and informal manner, their eyes burning brighter as their pupils widened with desire, their mouths curved into secretive smiles.

Collette clutched my arm. "Quincey . . . What is happening?" she whispered uncertainly.

"They're just making themselves more comfortable for the entertainment to come," I explained, gently drawing her forward. I had caught sight of someone I wanted to speak with. "Aunt Rosemary!" I called across the room. "How good to see you." I'd had no opportunity to greet Rosemary before dinner—she'd arrived at table late and had then been placed at the opposite end. I crossed the rug toward her now, Collette still at my side.

Rosemary held out her arms. "Hello, my handsome boy," she said fondly.

Smiling at her words, I went into her embrace. "Are you quite well?" I asked her.

But before Rosemary could reply, Collette tugged anxiously at my arm. "Everyone is looking at me, Quincey," she said. "Why do they seem so . . ." Collette fell silent as she watched the transformations taking place around her.

I glanced at Father, standing beside Mother before the great fireplace. Their eyes now glittered as red as the ruby wine in their crystal goblets. I sensed the onlookers lean forward, their expectancy infusing the room with excitement.

"To Quincey!" Father toasted, holding up his glass to me. He gave a proud smile, his still-perfect white fangs now fully descended.

Beside me, Collette gasped. I felt her nails dig into my arm as the rest of the room followed my father's example. Alarm had seized her. "Please, I'd—I'd like to go back to my room," she begged.

"Collette, darling, there is nothing to concern yourself about," I replied softly. "They're just interested in you, that's all. They enjoy new company. You wouldn't deprive them." I lifted her chin so that she stared up into my eyes. "Look at me, sweet one . . ." I crooned. I drew her into my gaze, mesmerizing her. Soon I felt her relax against me.

"That's better," I whispered.

I ran my fingers up her slim, elegant arms and then began to stroke the nape of her neck. She shivered, exhaling deeply. I felt her breath penetrate the thin white material of my shirt. The warm smell of her blood was affecting me. I felt my hunger rise. I bent my face toward hers and she pressed against me, trembling, her mouth opening—inviting my kiss.

"Do you see why I didn't take you in the railway carriage?" I murmured. "This will be so much better."

"Oh yes, Quincey . . ." she gasped.

I flicked my gaze once more to Father and Mother and saw them watching proudly from the fireplace. In a moment I would be like them—fully vampire. My heart swelled. And then I lowered my mouth to Collette's.

She grasped me with both hands, pulling me wantonly against her. I traced a line of kisses along her jaw and down her throat, feeling for the richest vein with the tip of my tongue. She arched her neck, groaning with desire, oblivious now to our audience. I felt the familiar tingling in my mouth as my fangs descended and sharpened. My own blood pounded in my ears— and then . . . I pressed the needle-sharp points in hard, shuddering with pleasure as I felt them puncture the soft, warm flesh. Blood flooded into my mouth, bathing my tongue, sending me heady. Mortal blood was like nothing I had ever tasted. Like the finest wine, it radiated through me, suffusing me with life.

Collette sighed, little mews of pleasure-pain. From somewhere beyond, I heard cheering and shouting.

I drank until Collette fell limp and gasping in my arms. Mindful that I should not continue until her heart stopped beating, I let her slip to the floor and wiped my mouth.

Father crossed the room and gripped my shoulders, then lifted my arm and turned me slowly around for the audience, as though I were a newly crowned champion. "On this, the most glorious of nights, my firstborn son has embarked on his destiny!" he announced. "We shall rule, as was intended, again!"

The roar of approval in the room grew almost deafening.

I looked down at Collette, lying there at my feet. She was still gasping, her eyes glazed. The world around me seemed suddenly fragile, while I had become mighty. A servant came to take Collette away. She would be thrown to the wolves.

Father then signaled for silence and the guests obediently obliged. "We must be patient now, my friends," he ordered. "Quincey has come into his power—but for destiny to be fully fulfilled, we must wait for his betrothed to reach womanhood."

He paused to gaze around the room at rapt faces, hungry for more rousing words. A smile stretched across his fangs. "Rosemary's daughter shall continue the bloodline, uniting both branches of our family tree."

Across the room, Rosemary gasped. She ran toward Father.

"No! No, please," she begged. "Not my daughter!"

Quick as a flash, Mother crossed the room. She held Rosemary back, laughing cruelly. "You little fool, the moment you came here, both of your children belonged to the house of Dracul."

"Father?" I asked, fixing him with a questioning gaze.

"My son," he said, clasping my shoulder. "You have a half brother—Rosemary's son, John Shaw. In the fullness of time, he shall be your brother in arms—and his sister, Lily, shall be your bride."

He turned once more to address the room. "And when that time comes, Quincey shall claim her!" he thundered. "To sire a new and stronger bloodline!"

CHAPTER 3

Journal of
Captain Quincey Harker

NORTHERN FRANCE
28TH JUNE 1916

How Father would love these killing fields! What a war this is—with prey sitting helpless, only yards away, herded together in trenches like cattle in an abattoir. I have only to wait for darkness and to follow the scent of fear.

I raided the enemy lines alone again last night. What joy it is to slip into the trench, sword drawn, and spray the walls with blood. My uniform was sodden with it. Its iron tang filled the air, stronger even than cordite from the shelling.

Rumor of my hunger must now be rife in the German trenches, for the smell of fear that lingers on my victims seems deep-seated in a way it never used to be—as if they have long dreaded my coming, standing guard, staring into the shadows of no-man's-land, knowing I may be on my way. . . .

This place will provide a splendid testing ground for John. I have arranged for him to join me here—though he, of course, knows nothing of my involvement in his posting. I am relishing the prospect of meeting my half brother at last. I shall take great pleasure in introducing him to the bloodlust that lies dormant within him, to guiding him toward his destiny.

Though I feel the old languor that follows a feast, I have changed into a clean uniform. I must make my inspection of the men before I sleep—and should now hurry, as dawn is fast approaching. . . .

THE ARMY AND NAVY CLUB
36–39 PALL MALL, LONDON
24TH SEPTEMBER 1916

I met my future wife today.

Lily came to John's bedside at the sanatorium while I was there. I must admit I was not prepared for her quiet charm, her cloud of dark curls, the flushes of rose in her cheeks, the serene blue of her eyes. Her features are no match for the exquisite splendor of Rebecca's, of course. But sweet and affecting nonetheless.

There is an air of such innocence about Lily. Looking down into her open, trusting face, I saw immediately that her heart will be oh so easy to capture.

She politely invited me to stay at Carfax Hall—but her clear gaze shone with a more intimate invitation, one that she herself almost certainly had no awareness she was making. I suppose it simplifies the affair—though a part of me yearns for more challenge.

Perhaps that is where the pleasure is to be found . . . in bringing out the wanton in one so pure. Yes, that indeed might be fun.

And so I have arranged to move my belongings to Carfax Hall tomorrow. It should be easy to lure Lily to Transylvania in plenty of time for the Saint Andrew's Eve feast. And where she goes, her loving brother, John, is bound to follow . . .

John—what a disappointment he has been. I expected to feel a kinship for him from the moment we met, but he has proved weak-willed, easily influenced, and ineffectual.

Father will no doubt be displeased at their first meeting. But perhaps once he is at the castle, John will discover and embrace his true nature.

CARFAX HALL

14TH OCTOBER 1916

This evening's dinner was one of enforced formality, as Lily had invited the very proper Miss Mary Seward to join us.

The name Seward at first sounded familiar to me. I

thought perhaps she was one of our kind, but that thought was entirely misguided.

Miss Seward is nursing John in the sanatorium—and she is transparent in her disapproval of me.

When our visitor had left, I could not resist defying her by playfully pulling Lily into my arms. She responded with such abandon, however, that I would have bitten the silly girl then and there but for my promise to Father that I would wait for Saint Andrew's Eve and our wedding night.

It took some strength of will to leave Lily at her bedroom door. I confess I am finding this part of Father's plan harder than I expected. Lily's innocent, trembling ardor, her open adoration—they fire such desire in me. . . . But I shall adhere to Father's wishes.

As I walked away, I was more relieved than surprised to find Dora, the maid, loitering in the darkened hallway in the erroneous belief that she couldn't be seen. The girl had been flirting with me since I arrived here, sending me little sideways glances when she brought fresh towels to my room, brushing against me when she bent to serve me at dinner. Her voice had a rough twang, but her face was pretty enough. "Were you spying on us, Dora?" I challenged her softly.

She started like a surprised cat and crept out from the shadows. "N-no, sir!" she gasped.

I scented fear on her, and it only served to stoke the

hunger that Lily had already aroused in me. I walked slowly toward her, and all the while she gazed down at the floor, clearly abashed at being caught. "Oh, I think you were," I said. "Do you often spy on your mistress and me?"

"Course not, sir!" she cried, twisting her hands together.

"Come now, Dora," I chided. "Why else would you be hiding here in the shadows at such a late hour?"

"I was takin' laundry to the airin' cupboard before I retired for the night," she mumbled.

"And where is this airing cupboard?" I pressed.

Dora glanced guiltily over her shoulder, back down the corridor.

"Nowhere near Miss Lily's room," I said, enjoying her discomfort. "So you tell falsehoods as well as spy on your employer?"

"I'm sorry, sir," Dora replied. "It's just that Miss Lily, she seems so diff'rent since you've been 'ere. An' I wondered . . ."

I lifted her chin with gentle fingers. Her skin was soft and warm. "You wondered what it was that had changed her," I finished for her. "Would you like me to show you?"

She looked up at me then. "Whatever do you mean, sir?" she asked. She pretended to be shocked—but there was a bold challenge in her gaze.

I pulled her to me. "Lily's mentioned your flirtatious ways," I murmured, and bent to kiss her. She opened her mouth to me immediately. I felt my eyes begin to burn, so kept them half closed. "Where is your room?" I murmured. "I shall see you safely there."

"That's kind, sir—I'll show you," Dora said with a triumphant little smile.

She led me back along the hall and up a narrow flight of stairs that led to the attic rooms. "This is mine," she announced proudly, stopping outside a white-painted door. She turned the handle and entered.

I followed her in. Moonlight shone through the room's tiny dormer window. The room was sparsely furnished with a narrow iron bedstead and a plain wardrobe and bedside table. The only splash of frivolity was a gaudily-feathered straw hat on a hook beside the wardrobe.

Dora hurried to the bedside table and lit the candle placed there. The bare walls flickered with its weak light. She blew out the match and sat down on the bed.

"Much more cozy . . ." I murmured, sitting down next to her. I ran a finger along the nape of her neck, feeling her shiver with anticipation, and then trailed it down her bosom, over her waist, and down to the hem of her skirt. The petticoats beneath felt cool and crisp.

She leaned into me, and I felt her soft, rounded form heave against me.

But even as I laid her down on the bed, I found that my mind, irritatingly, was filled with Lily. How I wished it were Lily with me, letting out tiny moans of pleasure. With a growl that came from deep within, I gripped Dora's throat in my teeth and penetrated the soft, pulsing flesh.

She stiffened and gasped, now staring up into my face—her own a mask of terror as she looked into my blazing eyes. Then her sweet blood flooded into my mouth, and her expression began to change again—this time to one of wonder. She clasped me to her and held me that way until I was sated.

I shall take Dora again when my desire for Lily grows unendurable, for I am determined to preserve Lily's innocence until the time is right.

But being with Dora—being with anyone but Lily now, I suspect—is like slaking my thirst with cheap beer when I crave a champagne that will sparkle on my tongue and send me heady with joy. . . .

15TH OCTOBER 1916

I did not think Dora such a weakling. The silly girl fainted while serving breakfast this morning. Lily was quite concerned about her. She sent her back to bed and called in the doctor, who said she might be anemic. I must have drawn more blood than I thought.

Dora later emerged, insisting she should serve us at dinner—even though it was supposed to be her night off—to make up for not working during the day, she said. Antanasia just shrugged, clearly prepared to let her get on with it.

But Lily protested. "Dora, you still look so pale and drawn. I do hope that you are not worried you might lose your position. Of course you won't!"

I do find myself shockingly moved by Lily's tenderness of spirit. After all I have seen and done in my life, to be affected so is surely ridiculous?

Despite Lily's reassurances, Dora remained reluctant to leave us. "I'm feelin' quite recovered, honest, Miss Lily," she insisted. "I'm 'appy to wait on you an' Mr. Harker." Her gaze drifted desperately toward me as she spoke.

"Go back to bed, Dora," I commanded, fearing she might betray her desire to Lily with such indiscreet glances. "We don't want you fainting again."

"Very well, sir, I shall . . ." she replied. She shot me a hopeful smile, her eyes glittering invitingly. The girl's imprudence sent a bolt of rage stabbing through my chest. I frowned at her then—and glanced at Lily, hoping she had not sensed the meaning in Dora's tone.

But Lily was still smiling sweetly at Dora, unheeding of Dora's betrayal. "Good," she said. "Rest is what you need, Dora."

As Dora left the room, I fought the urge to sigh out loud with relief. "Dear Lily," I murmured softly, placing my hand over hers.

When it was time to retire for the night, I left Lily with the most innocent of kisses and then went straight to Dora's room.

She was not there, and neither were her coat and hat. Fortunately, she had made it easy for me to preserve appearances.

I quickly cleared out her drawers and wardrobe, packing her few things into a suitcase that I concealed temporarily beneath my bed. And then I slipped out of the house and down the drive in search of her.

I spied her through the window of the local public house, leaning against the bar and drinking with another woman I supposed to be her sister. She had the same wide mouth and turned-up nose.

It was past closing time—I knew I wouldn't have to wait long. A few minutes later the two women, along with the other malingerers, were ejected by the landlord.

With a raucous laugh, the sister thrust an arm through one of the men's and they began to walk back toward the village. I watched as Dora turned and began to make her way alone back toward Carfax Hall.

Silently I caught up with her. "I've been looking for you," I murmured, falling into step alongside her.

She turned around in fright, her face then alighting in pleasure as she recognized me. "Oh . . . Mr. Harker! I thought I'd slip out for a few glasses of stout. I'm told it builds the blood," she slurred sheepishly. "And there I was, fearing you'd done with me, the way you frowned at me when I turned out to serve dinner."

"Oh no, Dora," I replied smoothly. "I'm not done with you at all."

"Let's walk back along the riverbank, then," she suggested, boldly tucking her arm through mine. "It's nice and secluded."

"Sounds perfect," I responded.

It seemed a shame not to take what was being offered. And it was pleasant enough, feeding on Dora there at the water's edge, moonlight rippling through the trees. When I felt her pulse begin to flutter and grow faint, I withdrew— though she begged deliriously for me to continue. I had no intention of draining her, however; I did not want the likes of her brought over to the darkness.

I plunged her head beneath the river's shimmering surface and held it there until her frantic struggles ceased. I left her there, in a manner of death befitting one so low.

If I had kept her alive, she could have satisfied my appetite for many a night to come. But she had become a liability. Her lack of discretion could have jeopardized everything.

How will I now resist Lily without any outlet for my desire? As I write, I imagine her, gently breathing in her warm bed, her dark curls strewn across her pillow. . . .

I must remain strong. I must remember my destiny.

21ST OCTOBER 1916

John came home from the sanatorium yesterday to complete his recovery at Carfax Hall. And now that wretched Seward girl has begun to visit him here! She was bothersome enough when she came here to visit Lily—making her disapproval of me clear. But pleasingly, my intended seems completely unswayed by Miss Seward's negativity.

It appears I have already won Lily's heart. Miss Seward's struggle against me is utterly in vain.

THE HOPE AND ANCHOR INN,
WHITBY
4TH NOVEMBER 1916

I have commenced the journey to Castle Dracula with Lily.

I used my connections in the Foreign Office to call John to London. They kept him busy long enough for me to get Lily away from Carfax Hall. As for Lily, she was easy to persuade. I told her I had been summoned back to Romania—that there was no time to lose and that I did not know when I would be back. Her initial distress soon dissolved when I followed the news with a proposal of marriage—and the request that she accompany me, Antanasia journeying with us for propriety's sake, of course. . . .

In such a state of giddy euphoria, Lily gratefully accepted my help in composing a letter to John, informing him of developments—and of where we are headed. For he shall, of course, follow us to Castle Dracula—just as the family wants him to. And then, without a backward glance, Lily left all she had known and followed me out of Purfleet.

Her trust in me, while foolish, is strangely moving. She is currently unaware of the fate that awaits her, but I have become determined to see that she is treated well at the castle and with the respect and deference my bride deserves.

We traveled here, to the northern port of Whitby, by train and tomorrow shall set sail for Varna. Once we arrive in Bulgaria, the rest of our journey, overland to Transylvania, should prove straightforward enough.

CASTLE DRACULA
24TH NOVEMBER 1916

Lily seemed so pleased when Mother pronounced her "magnificent." I was glad Lily did not understand all that lay behind the compliment. . . .

Our plan is falling into place. John has arrived at the castle.

There is only one fly in the ointment—he has brought with him that wretched Seward girl. I must decide what to do with her. . . .

It is nearly done. Mother has seduced John and made him fully vampire. He is one of us now. After my marriage to Lily tonight, the future of the Tepes bloodline will be assured.

This final entry is a farewell to the existence I have known.

Lily is dead. All is lost.

Without her by my side, I cannot lead the house of Tepes as Father intended.

I am done with this place. John may inherit it all.

I still reel from his callous acceptance of Lily's death. "She has proved herself weak. We are stronger without her." His own sister! Has he no vestige of his mortal self left?

I pity those he will rule. Though my heart may be shadowed, his has fast become blacker than the night. I am awed by the speed of the change in him.

I introduced John to his true bloodline. And in so doing, I have unleashed a monster on the world. We have all paid a dear price in Father's attempt to regain power.

Except, that is, for the one person who somehow slipped away unscathed—Mary Seward.

She thinks she has escaped and left the darkness behind.

But I will be seeing her sooner than she knows.

CHAPTER 4

*Journal of
John Shaw*

CASTLE DRACULA

1ST DECEMBER 1916

So . . .

Quincey was foolish not to have burned his journals before he left. My discovery of them has pleased me greatly. What I have read so far has been highly enlightening. I shall read them in their entirety, learn more of his weakness, while I bide my time and plan my revenge.

Long-lost brother.

Newfound enemy.

How dare he dismiss his own destiny—and in doing so dismiss me?

He condemns me as a monster? It is he who led me to this! He, who was given so much! He was coddled and supported, loved and indulged, celebrated for the vampire blood

48

he was born with—while I was separated from my family, left blind to my true heritage. He basked in both his own and my mother's affection—while I wept alone, believing her dead. He anticipated his first vampire bite as a rite of passage and savored its sweetness when it came. My initiation was thrust upon me without warning. I was seduced by the lies and depravity of his mother.

And then, after luring me to Castle Dracula so that I would discover the devastating truth of my own true nature—he destroyed Tepes before I could even acknowledge him as my father.

Thanks to Quincey, my first sight of Tepes was to be my last. Our father was writhing in agony upon the stone floor of his quarters, blood frothing at his lips as he clawed at the wooden stake Quincey had thrust through his heart!

I watched Quincey turn away and walk toward the door.

Gathering myself, I protested. "You brought me here. You helped unleash my true nature. And now you are abandoning me?"

He did not deny it. "I gave you what was rightfully yours," he called back. "It is up to you what you do with it."

I followed him down the staircase and watched him stride across the entrance hall toward his own wing of the castle, his footfalls ringing out on the marble floor.

"You can have it all, John!" he shouted. With a great sweep of his arms, he gestured to the paintings and weaponry displayed on the soaring stone walls around us. "I want none of it anymore."

I wish I'd had to strength to kill him there and then.

But I know where he is going. And in time, I shall have the strength I need.

I have discovered the family archive here in the castle library. It will teach me all I need to know of what a real Tepes should be. I shall tutor myself in all the ways of darkness and become strong—as strong as Quincey.

I shall have my vengeance on him—and all who try to interfere.

Yes. I shall make Quincey pay for betraying his bloodline—for walking away from his duty, killing our father, abandoning me. . . .

I will be his judge, his jury, and his executioner.

CHAPTER 5

*Journal of
Mary Seward*

I visited Grace today. Her parents were holding a small party to celebrate her second birthday. Today is the date we chose for her, knowing she was around three months old when I rescued her and brought her to England a year and nine months ago.

The maid showed me into the Edwardses' parlor, bright with the morning sun. I smiled at the balloons and streamers put up for Grace, who was running happily around the room, her face lit up with excitement while her adoptive mother and father looked on fondly.

Seeing me enter, Andrew and Jane immediately came over.

"Look who it is, Gracie! Aunt Mary has come to see you!" Andrew called.

Grace came running and flung her arms around my legs. I swept her up and kissed her, then swung her around. She laughed gleefully, and the sound filled me with joy.

To me, it still seems like a gift from God that I found a local Purfleet couple to adopt Grace and so soon after I escaped from Transylvania with her. There had been times in Castle Dracula when I believed I would never see home again. The horrors of that place will haunt me forever, but Grace, being just a baby when she was imprisoned there, will have escaped unscathed in mind as well as body, God willing.

How wonderful it was to see Purfleet unchanged when I arrived back here with Grace on Christmas Eve, 1916. And how much more so to discover that my darling father still lived! The illness that had threatened to take him while I was away had not yet conquered him. Tears of relief ran down my cheeks as I stood at his bedside.

He looked at me in wonder—and then at Grace in my arms.

"I saved her from them," I told him. "She was stolen from the village below the castle for Tepes. He was to drink her blood so that he would have the strength to attend Quincey and Lily's wedding ceremony."

Father's eyes darkened with grim understanding. Many years before I was born, he, too, had faced the evil in the castle. He, too, had survived to tell the tale.

"Baby's blood is the most powerful vampiric rejuvenator," he said somberly, holding out a finger for Grace to grasp. "Her parents are dead?"

I nodded.

"If she was born in that village, she would have been baptized the moment she was born," Father went on. "But now, having been so close to evil, she should be blessed again—and soon."

"I shall ask Reverend Halifax in the morning," I assured him.

Christmas morning arrived crisp and sunny—and blanketed in pure white. It had snowed heavily during the night. I wrapped Grace up well, kissed Father goodbye, and then trudged through the village with Grace in my arms toward the parish church. The gleaming whiteness all around seemed to bring with it a sense of peace. Purfleet felt like a place of purity and light—a world away from the dark, hellish place from which we had escaped. In the distance, the church bells began to peal out their Christmas salutation.

My muffled footsteps crunched up the churchyard path. The way was crowded with cheery parishioners arriving for the morning service. Such a scene seemed unreal after the horrors I had witnessed. I felt suddenly disoriented and out of place—light-headed and overwhelmed by so many faces. The blissful peace that had enfolded me grew brittle and seemed to crack like ice struck with a hammer. My heart began to pound and my palms to sweat.

Some called, "Merry Christmas!" as I passed, but I found myself unable to meet a gaze or return a greeting. Others stared curiously and nudged each other. I was uncomfortably aware of the gossip and speculation I, a young lady returning from Europe with a baby in my arms, might provoke. Before my ordeal, I would have raised my head boldly, but now my nerve failed me. I stared straight ahead, trying to quell my rising panic, overwhelmed by the press of people.

"Mary!" Reverend Halifax's familiar voice broke through the maelstrom. I looked over to see him standing at the church door, welcoming the arrivals, and hurried toward him.

"You're back among us at last," he said with a smile. "And you bring a new lamb into our fold." He beamed down at Grace, lying peacefully in my arms.

I told him only that Grace was an orphan from war-ravaged Europe. Without hesitation he promised to bless her during the service and, gratefully, I carried Grace into the church.

Sunlight shone through the stained-glass windows, spreading a kaleidoscope of glorious color across the aisle and altar. The pews were already half filled. Bright bonnets and scarves had been brought out for the occasion. I smelled the fresh garden scent of the scarlet poinsettias arranged around the stone pillars.

"Look," I whispered to Grace as I carried her to the front pew to await the moment Reverend Halifax would call us to the altar. "This is how joyful and good life can be."

I spoke to reassure myself as much as her, but as I settled upon the smooth wood of the pew, a passing cloud snuffed out the streams of colored light. A shiver of remembrance cut cruelly through my hard-won optimism. I was cast back to the gloomy church in Transylvania where I'd sought holy water to protect John and me in our rescue mission to Castle Dracula. How grateful I had been for the small comfort of that dismal place, for the glass vials of holy water the priest had given me. I'd prayed they would be enough to help us save Lily.

But they had not been.

We had not saved her.

Indeed, I had lost John too, my sweet, loving fiancé.

I tried not to imagine him as he was now, lost to the darkness. But it was impossible to forget the demonic, heartless creature he'd become. Tears welled in my eyes, grief mingling with fear. I clutched Grace closer to me and prayed that I'd never see John or his black-hearted half brother, Quincey Harker, ever again. Nor any of their kind.

"At least I was able to save you, Grace," I murmured. "God willing, we'll be safe here."

The moment came for the reverend to call me to the altar with Grace. I felt a sense of calm descend once more as he intoned the words of blessing over her.

As I turned to return to my pew, I noticed a young woman staring at the bundle in my arms. The sunlight lit her curly golden hair like a halo as she leaned forward in her seat to get a better view of Grace.

After the service she approached me, accompanied by an anxious-looking man. I met the woman's gaze and smiled an invitation.

She leaned forward and gently drew back the knitted blanket that screened Grace's face. "What a dear little mite . . ." she breathed, a note of such wistfulness in her voice. "I'm afraid we haven't been blessed with one of our own," she added quietly.

She looked up at me and smiled, but her eyes glistened with tears. I saw the man, whom I now took to be her husband, squeeze her arm supportively.

Jane and Andrew Edwards, I learned, were a loving couple stricken with sorrow that they could have no children of their own. It seemed the most natural thing in the world to give them Grace. I was far too young and inexperienced to care for her myself. And more, it soothed my heart when Father mentioned approvingly that their family name of Edwards meant "blessed guardian." It seemed an omen— though no one, least of all the Edwardses, would ever guess the terrible truth of how Grace came to be orphaned and brought to England.

The legalities of Grace's adoption were simply solved, for

Andrew is a solicitor. And on the twelfth day of Christmas, it was they who carried Grace to the altar for her to be baptized as their own dear child.

I stood as godmother. And as I renounced all evil and promised to protect Grace and help her to take her place within the life and worship of God's church, I felt my insides tremble. Would I be strong enough to keep such a promise? I alone, among those gathered there, had encountered some of the true evils of which the reverend spoke.

I protected her once, I thought. If need be, I shall do so again. But I prayed that neither Grace, nor her new family, would ever need to know of the horrors from which I'd rescued her. . . .

Seeing Grace today, now two years old, beloved and safe, brought me such joy. Jane asked me to stay for dinner, and part of me longed to linger within the warmth and cheeriness of the Edwardses' home. But I had to refuse, of course, in order to get home before dark. Since my return from Transylvania, the darkness frightens me more than it did when I was a child. Back then, I only suspected monsters lurked there. Now I know they truly do.

As it was, the sun was already a low fiery ball in the sky as I set off along the empty lane. My pulse began to quicken. I despise the restless anxiety I feel as twilight approaches.

As sun sank lower on the horizon, I clasped both my crucifix and a small vial of holy water, each worn on a chain around my neck—clinging to the symbols of religion like a drowning man clings to driftwood.

Only the horizon retained its pale light as the sun swiftly began to set. Dead leaves swirled about my feet as I hurried along the trail. In my mind, their noise turned into the swish of vampire wings. The howling wind echoed the sound of the wolves surrounding Castle Dracula.

My heart hammered in my chest, and I picked up my pace, my eyes darting left and right, searching the night for the slightest hint of movement. I glanced behind. Out of the corner of my eye, I glimpsed a shadow, hulking and broad.

"Who is there?" I shouted. The figure remained impassive.

I gasped, convinced it was the outline of a vampire, lurking there. Lying in wait for me!

Fresh terror coursed through me like electricity. My alarm spiraled into panic as I broke into a run, my coat fluttering behind me. I had only to turn the corner and I would be in view of home—but my breathing was so fast I felt light-headed. Sparks of light began to flash before me. I feared I would faint there on the lane.

Sucking in great gulps of air, I battled to outrun my panic and reach the gate. I pelted through, leaving it swinging on its hinges. My feet sent the gravel flying as I raced along the path to the door, fumbling in my bag for my key.

What was that noise behind me? I could not look. My heart felt it would burst as my shaking fingers desperately tried to fit the key into the lock. At last they found pur-chase. I flung open the door and fell inside, slamming it behind me.

Leaning against it, I drew the bolt, then glanced grate-fully at the small crucifix facing the door.

Relief made me weak. As I slid into the chair beside the coat stand, my chest heaved with sobbing and I fought to stifle it lest Father hear me.

Eventually, somewhat calmer, I forced myself to look out of the hallway window. The garden stood quiet and empty.

There was neither a vampire nor anything there in the darkness that so terrified me. Once more, fear and anxiety had misled my senses.

I have seen or heard nothing of John or Quincey Harker since returning to England. And yet even now, as I write in the safety of my room, I am governed by my fear of them.

I pray that I shall one day be free from the tyranny of it.

EXETER NEWS

26TH SEPTEMBER 1918

BODY DISCOVERED NEAR DOCKS

The dead body of an unknown woman was dis-covered in an alley near the docks last night. The victim had been subjected to a brutal attack. Her body was found by Mrs. Irene Baverstock, proprietor of the nearby Bell Inn. Mrs. Baverstock told our reporter, "I could see she'd been used most vilely by the torn clothing and all the blood. We often have a bit of trouble by the docks when a new ship is in, but never nothing as shocking as this before."

No clue has been found as to the identity either of the victim or her murderer—or as to the motive. Police believe from the victim's apparel and the substantial contents discovered in her purse that she was what is termed in polite circles a "lady of the night."

*Journal of
Mary Seward*

PURFLEET

26TH SEPTEMBER 1918

I have just awoken from dreaming of John again. . . .

He lay in his hospital bed as first I'd seen him, pale and vulnerable, needy of my care and affection. I held his hand

and cooled his brow with kisses, and he opened clear blue eyes to gaze at me—as though at an angel.

"John . . ." I breathed. "You've come back to me."

"My darling Mary," he replied, "how could you think I would abandon you?"

And then, gently, he pulled me to him and kissed me, so tenderly it filled my heart anew with love for him.

Gradually his hold on me tightened, its strength taking me by surprise. I tried to draw away to see if anything was wrong, but John would not let me. He began to laugh—and the inhuman sound of it chilled me to the core.

At last, he loosened his grip enough for me to pull back and see his face . . . to take in the reddened, staring eyes, the leering, fanged mouth. I began to scream—but silently, the noise never leaving my mouth. All the while, I watched that monstrous orifice coming toward my throat, its upper lip curling back to expose the full savagery of its two needle-sharp fangs. . . .

I awoke, as I always do, drenched in sweat and panic—and with a feeling of such sorrow.

To recall so vividly the John that was—to remember such love and then realize anew that it is lost to me forever . . . it seems so cruel. I am forced to mourn afresh as he transforms in my dreams to the fiend he is now—tainted by evil, beyond love, faithful only to his own bloodlust.

Though strongest at night, my fear of the darkness never really leaves me. It prickled in my fingers as I fastened the present I had bought for Grace's birthday around her chubby wrist—a silver bangle, marked with the sign of the cross.

Will I ever again feel truly safe?

I pray to God that I will. But so far, that prayer has gone unanswered.

CHAPTER 6

Journal of
Quincey Harker

They hunt me. I know they hunt me. But they will not find me here. The cavernous dark of the catacombs beneath the city of Exeter shall conceal me. For who apart from the rats would dare enter the dank shadows of such a place?

The city rats are different from those that inhabited the wartime trenches: less fat and sleek. There are no fallen men for them to gorge on here—or for me, either. The only sustenance to be had is the water that drips slowly from the curved stone ceilings. It is not enough, of course. My soul howls for blood.

There was scarce enough to draw from such a tiny helpless creature, but sufficient to sustain me as I bide my time.
Soon I shall seek out Mary Seward.

I should never have let her go.

*Journal of
Mary Seward*

30TH SEPTEMBER 1918

I was late for my shift at the sanatorium this morning; I had
to wait for Mrs. Frobisher to arrive. Seven o'clock came and
went with no sign of her, but I won't leave Father unat-
tended. I was very glad to see her when she finally came
hurrying around the corner into view.

"Sorry, miss," she puffed, sweeping through the front door
and unfastening her hat. "My youngest had croup and I was
up most of the night tending to her."

"Not to worry," I assured her. "I do hope little Amy is
fully recovered?"

Mrs. Frobisher nodded gratefully. She has such a
large family, I sometimes wonder how she finds the time

and energy to come to us as well as tend to all their needs.

I am forever appreciative that she agrees to remain the day as nurse and companion to Father once her housekeeping duties are completed, thus freeing me to work at the sanatorium. Though he needs constant care himself, Father insisted that I resume my post there as a VAD nurse. "Wounded soldiers continue to arrive there and have far more acute need of your tender care than I, my dear," he told me. "I shall continue to muddle along with Mrs. Frobisher during the day and look forward to your company in the evenings."

Mrs. Frobisher has proved such a blessing. She nursed Father valiantly while I was away in Transylvania. The doctor seemed to think that he'd stubbornly hung on to life just to see me safely home. But in so doing, Father had rallied—and here he is, all this time later, still with us—though his health will always remain delicate.

I would find it so hard to entrust Father's care to someone other than Mrs. Frobisher now. Especially having heard Lily's tales of her treacherous guardian and housekeeper, Antanasia.

I am glad, though, that Father persuaded me to resume my VAD duties. The routine and sheer hard work at the sanatorium distract me from my anxieties for at least some of the day. And little by little, I have steeled myself to bear the sight of blood-stained bandages and drenched swabs. I remind myself that this is blood nobly spilt for king and country, not by evil vampires gorging on it out of greed and lust.

I have digressed. My thoughts wander so these days. I used to pride myself on my clear thinking. But now it is rare that I follow a thought from beginning to end without distraction. It must be the lack of rest. My nightmares continue to rob me of sleep. Where did I begin? Oh yes . . .

When Mrs. Frobisher finally arrived this morning, I hurried from the house and reached the sanatorium flustered and breathless from running. The ward gleamed in the autumn sunshine that flooded through the windows and bathed the long rows of beds in warm light. The astringent tang of antiseptic filled the air. A group of patients—those well enough to leave their beds—were seated around the table in the bay window, drinking tea from white enamel mugs and laughing and joking among themselves.

"I'm so sorry, Sister," I called across the ward, straightening my cap. "Mrs. Frobisher was late, and I couldn't leave Father. . . ."

Sister nodded curtly. "I trust this won't become a habit, Nurse Seward," she replied.

Sister detests lack of punctuality—she sees it as a lack of discipline.

"Fortunately, the new VAD nurse arrived on time," she added pointedly. Her sharp blue gaze flicked across the ward to a uniformed girl I hadn't seen before. She was bent over a bed, busily tucking in a neat, blanketed corner.

I felt my face burn with mortification. I had forgotten that a number of new VAD nurses were starting—and one of them was on my rota. It was my job to show her around and help her settle in.

Having finished the bed, the new nurse straightened and turned toward Sister with an eager smile, as though awaiting her next instructions.

"This is Nurse Mary Seward," Sister informed her. "You'll take orders from her—now that she's arrived. I have paperwork that needs attending to." And then she turned on her heel and swept into her office.

"All clear!" called one of the patients seated by the table. "At ease, everyone."

The other patients laughed heartily.

"Sergeant Hopkins!" I chided, but couldn't prevent a smile at his comment as I hurried past him to greet the new nurse.

She flashed me a rueful grin. "I think Sister must have got out of bed on the wrong side this morning," she said, holding out her hand. "Pleased to meet you, Mary. I'm Helen Pargeter."

"Glad to have you here, Helen," I said, taking her hand.

"Come on, Nurse Seward. You've got to admit Sister's a bit of a stickler," Sergeant Hopkins went on.

"But I bet under all that starched cotton, there beats a feisty heart!" Corporal Croft crowed.

"You're right, Crofty, and I bet you wouldn't mind loosenin' 'er apron a bit and findin' out." Corporal Tandy laughed.

I looked at Helen to see how she was taking their bawdy bantering, concerned she might be embarrassed. But she just rolled her eyes.

"I have brothers just like them," she told me with a grin. "It's all talk. Besides, Stella and Becky mentioned there were some shenanigans last night, so I was prepared for these troublemakers today."

"Stella and Becky?" I echoed, confused.

"I share digs with them. They're new VADs too," Helen explained. "They both had their first shift last night, and we had a brief chat when they arrived home." Mischievously she winked over my shoulder at Hopkins. "They warned me about you, Sergeant, and I'll be having none of your tomfoolery."

I smiled, pleased to find my new colleague so good-natured.

A clatter at my back made me start and I spun around to see Sergeant Hopkins sprawled, laughing, on the floor. "Sorry, Nurse Seward!" he shouted as the other soldiers cheered and whistled at him. "One of these days I'll get the hang of these damned crutches."

Helen and I hurried toward him to help him to his feet. "For goodness' sake, be careful, Sergeant!" I called anxiously. "We don't want your wound to open again!"

LATER

"A new face!" Father smiled that night when I told him about Helen's arrival. "Good, good. Let's hope she becomes a friend as well as a colleague. It's high time you got out a bit and had some fun."

I nodded but could not help frowning down at my needlepoint. Dear Father. I know he worries about me and fears my life has become too secluded. I wish I could go back to being the spirited, cheerful daughter I used to be. But how can I after all I have seen?

I must finish writing now and try to get some rest— try not to think of the night beyond my closed curtains that makes panic rise and fall in my breast like the sea pounding on the shore. How envious I am of people who still go about their lives, free from the iron grip of such nighttime terrors, blissfully unaware of the horrors that stalk the earth in the hours of darkness.

EXETER NEWS

3RD OCTOBER 1918

LOCAL CHILD MISSING

Nine-year-old Sarah Harding went missing yesterday evening. She had been sent by her mother to fetch eggs from Harborough Farm but did not arrive home again. As darkness fell, her worried father and brother went out to look for her and found the upturned egg basket in the ditch alongside the farm track. Of Sarah herself, there was no sign.

If anyone has any information about the girl's whereabouts or finds any items they think might belong to her, please contact Constable Morley at Chilcomb Police Station.

Sarah has light brown hair. She is described as a slight girl, not tall for her age, with brown eyes. She was wearing a red shawl, a blue-striped smock over a brown cotton dress, black stockings, and brown boots.

CHAPTER 7

*Journal of
Mary Seward*

Tonight at dinner, as Father's unsteady hand brought his wineglass to his mouth, a trickle of its ruby red contents spilled down onto his beard.

I leaned forward to dab the crimson spots from his mouth with my napkin and then stared down at the red stains; so like John's blood-soiled collar after Mina Harker had bitten him. . . .

Father must have realized the drift of my thoughts, for he reached out and squeezed my hand. "Mary, my dear," he began, "I understand your fear. I have been aware of it since you returned. Like you, I know that once one has seen the face of evil, it is impossible to drive it completely from one's mind. We both now share the certainty that it exists, and in a form more dark and cruel than we could ever have imagined." His voice was quivering and breathless, weakened by infirmity and emotion, but he pressed on. "However, it must not stop us from *living*. Knowing it exists cannot make the evil stronger—it must make *us* stronger."

His heartfelt words awoke in me an urge to confide the feelings that had plagued me for so long. "But I don't feel strong, Father!" I cried, placing my hand over his. I bent my head, feeling tears well in my eyes. "I cannot bear knowing that such horror lurks out there."

"But Mary, my dear, you do have that strength. You have faced that horror and survived—and you must find it within yourself again," Father urged.

"But how?" I protested. "When the nightmares come, I am powerless to fight them!"

"You are not powerless!" Father's voice cracked as his eyes burned into mine. Was it anger I detected in his voice? I hadn't seen this kind of fire in him in years. "You have hidden away from the world since your return and indulged every hideous imagining," he scolded. "Your evenings are empty because you will not venture out. You shun society. Is it any wonder dark thoughts fill the void you yourself have created?"

His words stung me. "Of course I am reluctant to trust others!" I replied. "I gave my heart to John Shaw—only to find that beneath all his sweetness slumbered the soul of a fiend!" Tears streamed down my face now, but I did not try to hide them.

Father lifted his own napkin and, with no little effort, leaned forward to gently dab them away. "Oh, Mary," he whispered. "I too loved one who turned to the darkness. You remember, from my notes, Lucy Westernra? I worshiped her even while Dracula drained her blood and turned her into an evil harpy."

I nodded, feeling a prick of sorrow at the thought of his own loss. It was strange to imagine Father as a handsome young man, with a life before I existed, when now he was so old and fragile.

He went on. "Somehow I found the strength to turn my back on the evils I had witnessed and find your mother." His rheumy eyes lit up for a moment. "Elizabeth . . . I could not have loved another more than I loved her." He gave me a tender smile. "And you must do the same, Mary. What good is defeating the darkness if you do not then let yourself revel in the light?" He clutched my hands between his, and for a fleeting moment, I felt his old strength there.

My heart wavered. "You are right, Father. I know you are right," I replied.

"Then you will try?" he appealed. "You will go out into the world once more?"

I took a deep breath and then nodded. "I will accept the next invitation I receive," I promised, and resolved to do so, no matter how frightened I felt.

I was rewarded for my bravery by Father's smile.

"But I cannot leave you alone," I added. "I must find someone to care for you while I am away."

"You must not use me as an excuse any longer, Mary," Father chided. "Mrs. Frobisher can always sit with me."

"Not of an evening," I countered. "Her family has need of her then."

Father looked at me sternly. I think he feared I was still making excuses.

"I will find someone," I promised him earnestly.

He nodded. "Good," he said, letting go of my hands and turning back to his plate.

I only pray I shall be strong enough to carry out my pledge. For what if the next invitation calls me out after dark?

4TH OCTOBER 1918

Once more, I find myself sleepless in the early hours.

I was awakened, not by the bloodsucking demons that inhabit my dreams, but by the sound of sobbing.

I opened my eyes and spied the outline of a figure standing at the foot of my bed. Cold terror gripped my heart as I sat up, a scream frozen in my throat, grasping the crucifix and pendant at my neck.

The scent of sweet violet wafted over me. Shock hit me like cold water.

"Lily?" My voice was a hoarse whisper. How could it possibly be? Lily was dead. I had seen her broken body on the rocks beneath Castle Dracula.

I fumbled for a match and lit the lamp beside my bed.

She was still in her wedding dress, her tear-streaked cheek as white as its lace. Her dark curls fell around her face, spilling over her narrow shoulders so that she seemed like a nymph raised from the sea, tousled by wind and wave. I thought of the first time I'd seen her at Carfax Hall, rushing in from the garden, fresh-cheeked and windswept, hair tendriled by the rain.

How strangely beautiful she was then. How wildly lovely she appeared now.

She moved around the bed without speaking, seeming to glide like the ghost she must be. But I was not afraid. It was relief rather than fear that flooded my heart. Lily was here with me! Not broken or bloody, but whole.

"Lily?" I called to her softly again, fearful of scaring her away.

She made no reply as she turned and glided across the room to the window.

I saw with a gasp that the window was open. How could that be? I always locked it and checked it before I retired for the night. I pushed back the bedclothes, alarmed.

Lily turned back to face me, lifting her hands to her heart, her eyes dark pools of sorrow—just as they had been when I last saw her alive.

"Quincey," she whispered, tears streaming down her pale face.

As I watched, she climbed up onto the sill. "Lily! Don't!" I cried, horror rising in my chest.

"Quincey," she repeated, pointing out into the inky black night.

"No!" I shouted. I leapt from my bed and darted toward her. This was my chance to save her where I had failed before.

She closed her eyes and once again breathed, "Quincey . . ."

As she prepared to leap, I reached out to grab her hand and—

My stomach lurched. Suddenly it was me falling, not Lily! Falling down the steep wall of Castle Dracula.

I flailed in terror as the wind screamed past my ears, buffeting my face and tearing at my hair. Emptiness yawned beneath me. And then I saw the jagged rocks below, waiting to welcome me. . . .

I screamed.

And then, thank God, I awoke properly—to find myself bolting upright in bed. The other awakening had been a trick of the mind—a novel departure in my nighttime terrors.

I lay back again, panting, drenched in sweat, until the panic subsided a little. I had not dreamed of Lily before. And then, just to be sure, I threw off my covers and hurried to the window. Pulling back the curtain, I tried the latch. It was still locked.

I let the curtain fall into place, shivering as the cool night air pressed my damp nightgown against my skin.

It had all seemed so real. . . .

But it was just another nightmare.

I shall sleep no more tonight. As I write this, to while away the hours until dawn, my relief at waking up in the safety of my own room is mixed with fresh grief. Once again, I feel hit with the shock of Lily's terrible death and am appalled anew that her sweet innocence was to have been taken for her by the abominable Quincey Harker.

May God condemn his blackened soul.

Journal of Quincey Harker

4TH OCTOBER 1918

It is time to leave my dark hiding place and head for Purfleet. That is where she will have fled. Like a vixen returning to her lair.

I hope you are ready to receive me, Mary Seward.

I am coming for you.

Chapter 8

EXETER NEWS

5TH OCTOBER, 1918

CHILD FOUND ALIVE

Missing nine-year-old Sarah Harding was discovered shocked and disoriented but unharmed on the Pilgrim's Way yesterday morning. Mr. Henry Morgan spotted her while journeying to his work at Chilcomb Foundry. "I remembered the newspaper description of the missing wench and realized straightaway that this must be her," Mr. Morgan said. "So I put my coat around her and took her to the police station."

The girl could not account for her disappearance and seemed unwilling or unable to describe what had happened to her.

"It was like she was in a trance," PC Morley reported. "But when her mother arrived and hugged her, Sarah began to scream—like she'd woken from a nightmare, wailing over and over,

'His eyes! His red eyes!'"

It has been suggested that Sarah might have fallen into the ditch and concussed herself, catching her throat on bramble thorns as she did so, which would account for the one or two scratches found there.

"We're just thankful to have Sarah back, safe in the bosom of her family," her weeping mother said. "I shall never let her out of my sight again."

ANDREW AND JANE EDWARDS

BLANCHARD HOUSE

PURFLEET

ESSEX

7TH OCTOBER 1918

YOU ARE CORDIALLY INVITED TO BLANCHARD HOUSE
FOR DINNER AND DANCING.
SATURDAY THE 19TH OCTOBER, 7:30 P.M. UNTIL LATE.
RSVP

P.S. Dearest Mary, how pleased we would be if you could join us. We know it's difficult for you to leave your father alone but do hope you may find a kind soul to sit with him, for we are sure an evening out would be a good tonic for you. Do please come!

Warmest wishes,

Jane

Journal of Mary Seward

8TH OCTOBER 1918

There was post waiting for me when I arrived home. As is my habit, I opened it at the dinner table. I recognized the grocer's bill in its manila envelope. Father leaves such household matters to me entirely now. But the cream envelope that lay beside it was unusual. I receive so little personal correspondence these days, and I did not recognize the neat handwriting that spelled my name.

"It was delivered by hand," Father told me as I glanced at it. His eyes were bright with interest. "Do open it, Mary. I've wondered what it contains since the boy brought it this afternoon."

"What boy?" I asked suspiciously.

"Just some lad from the village," Father replied. "I had Mrs. Frobisher give him a ha'penny for his trouble."

I slowly slit open the envelope and drew out an invitation card to a dinner party at the Edwardses'. My appetite vanished. I had been rash to promise Father I would accept the next invitation I received.

Father must have seen the dismay on my face. "Not bad news, I hope?" he asked anxiously.

"An invitation to dinner," I murmured.

"Excellent!" He brightened at once. "You'll accept, of course."

"I have not yet found anyone to sit with you," I argued.

"Then you must do so," he answered firmly. "Or I shall simply spend the evening alone, for I will not be used as an excuse for you to avoid the world."

"I cannot leave you alone!" I gasped, alarmed at the very thought.

"Then what about asking that new nurse you mentioned?" Father insisted, undeterred. "She sounds like a good type."

"Yes, she is," I agreed reluctantly. He had found the perfect solution. Helen was trustworthy and reliable. And Father would likely enjoy her easygoing company. "Very well. I shall ask her," I told him, feeling my mouth go dry as I spoke the words.

"Good girl," Father said contentedly.

I gave him a weak smile.

She may have a prior engagement. She may decline, I

reassured myself as I pushed my remaining food around my plate.

I only hoped that would be the case.

LATER

Father is long asleep now, and my candle burns low. Apprehension grips me like a vise. If Helen agrees to my request, I will have no option but to accept the Edwardses' invitation. I cannot break my word to Father; he would be so disappointed in me.

I will have to face the darkness.

9TH OCTOBER 1918

What a long day it has been.

Nightmares of Castle Dracula kept me awake again last night. And this morning, as I stood before the mirror to pin up my hair for work, I was struck by my own haunted expression. It reminded me of one I have seen countless times at the sanatorium on the faces of patients freshly returned from the horror of the trenches. I know I can never truly imagine the physical agony the patients have suffered—continue to suffer—but I believe I understand something of the mental torment they endure.

Tiredness dragged at my limbs through my shift. I felt the very air heavy on me as I moved about the ward.

"You should go earlier to your bed, Seward," Sister chided when she caught me yawning.

"Yes, Sister," I mumbled. If only it were that simple, I thought as I watched her walk smartly off the ward. Wearily I prepared a tray of scissors, forceps, and bandages in readiness for the next round of dressing changes.

As I passed by Sergeant Hopkins's bed, the tray slipped from my fingers. Fatigue had made me clumsy and the instruments clattered to the floor, skidding in every direction.

A great cheer rose up among the men.

"Blimey, Seward—you'll be for it now!" Sergeant Hopkins teased as I crouched down and started to gather the instruments back onto the tray.

Helen hurried over and reached down for a bandage that had unrolled beneath Sergeant Hopkins's bed. "Here," she said, handing it to me. "We'll have this cleared up and another tray prepared before the doctor arrives. Sister doesn't even need to know—*does she, Sergeant Hopkins*?"

Sergeant Hopkins gave us both a wink and tapped his nose. "Not a word shall pass our lips, eh, lads?" he said with a grin.

The other patients good-naturedly called their agreement.

"Thanks, Helen," I murmured, greatly touched by her

kindness. Her efficiency smoothed my ragged nerves. On the spur of the moment, I decided I would ask her about sitting with Father.

"Helen," I began hesitantly, "I wondered if I might ask you a favor. . . ."

"Why, of course," Helen answered immediately. Indeed, she looked pleased to be asked. "What is it?"

"I have received a dinner invitation," I explained. "Left to me, I would decline it, as my father is in poor health and I don't like to leave him alone. But Father is insistent I go out and socialize . . ." I went on, feeling my lips break into a rueful smile. "So, I was hoping that you might consider sitting with him that evening. It's on the nineteenth."

Helen's face fell. "Oh, Mary, I would love to help you out, but . . ." She hesitated. "Johnny, my gentleman friend, returns from the front that day. I'm so—"

"No apologies. Of course you'll want to spend the evening with him," I excused her hurriedly, straightening the scissors on the tray beside me. Inwardly I heaved a sigh of relief.

"But maybe Stella or Becky could do it," Helen offered.

I swallowed hard. "Don't they both do night duties?"

"Well, it might be a night off for their rota." Helen fixed me in a playful grin. "They do sometimes get them, you know!"

"Of course," I muttered, disheartened.

"Why don't you come back with me after our shift and meet them?" Helen offered eagerly. "Stella especially might be keen to help you out—she hates staying in on her evenings off; she gets cabin fever shut up in our poky little house!"

I forced a grateful smile, aware I should not let my anxieties overwhelm good sense. "Well, if you're sure . . ." I replied. I had quickly grown comfortable in Helen's good-natured company; why shouldn't her friends be as reliable and trustworthy as she?

So, at the end of our shift, I accompanied Helen to the small house at the end of the village where she was boarding with Stella and Becky. She unlocked the front door with her key and bounded straight up the stairs calling, "Hello, there! I've brought a visitor!"

I followed her up the staircase, the flowery carpet soft under my feet, my coat brushing against the brightly painted banister.

Helen swung open the first bedroom door at the top of the stairs. "Stella?" she called.

"In the bath, darling!" a muffled voice called from behind a door.

Helen crossed the landing to another door. "Let's see if Becky's up yet—she should be if she isn't!" After a quick knock, she clicked it open. "Becky? Are you decent?"

"Helen! You're back already. Sure, come in." I heard

the lilting tone of a soft Irish brogue from within.

Helen beckoned me to follow as she slipped through the doorway. "I share this room with Becky," she whispered to me. "It's a bit of a squeeze, but it's cheaper to share."

Becky was up—but only just, I could see. She was still in her nightgown—which looked at least two sizes too big. She was kneeling in the narrow space beside her bed.

"I was just saying my prayers. Forgot to do it before I went to bed after my shift," she said a little sheepishly. "I just can't get used to this sleeping in the day. I don't know whether I'm coming or going!"

Helen went over and lit the gas lamp. Its warm glow illuminated the still-curtained room.

"Oh, that's better," Becky said, blinking like an owl. She reached clumsily toward her nightstand, feeling for a pair of spectacles that lay there. When she put them on, she looked even more owl-like, her eyes enlarged behind the thick lenses.

"Hello!" she said, suddenly noticing me and hastily smoothing back her mouse brown hair.

"This is Mary," Helen explained. "The nurse on my rota who's been teaching me the ropes."

"Mary!" Becky greeted me like an old friend. "How nice to meet you at last. Helen's told us all about you."

"Come and sit in front of the fire." Helen ushered me to the battered chair placed before the tiny iron fireplace in the far corner of the bedroom. Small flames flickered in the grate.

As Helen stooped to place a few more coals on, Becky quickly smartened her bed and shrugged into a tattered old dressing gown. Then she gasped. "Oh, I'd forget me head if it was loose, so I would!" She scooped up a small glass bottle from her bedside table, uncorked it, tipped a few drops of its clear contents onto her fingers, and crossed herself before sprinkling a few more drops on her bed.

I assumed it was scent, though I could not detect its smell. I stared in wonder.

Helen laughed affectionately. "It's holy water," she explained. "Becky's always dabbing herself with the stuff."

Becky looked momentarily embarrassed. "My ma's convinced this country is filled with boggarts and banshees and that evil is bound to prey on an innocent country girl like myself." She grinned and rolled her eyes. "I promised I'd keep myself doused in the holy water while I was away from home."

I smiled back. It was impossible not to warm to Becky, and I found myself comforted by her superstitious piety.

How interesting that at one time, I would have privately thought it foolish to put stock in such practices.

"Is it your first time in England?" I asked her.

"First time away from home anywhere," she told me, straightening her spectacles.

Just then, a door on the landing clattered open. The heady scent of an exotic perfume wafted into the room, followed by a strikingly beautiful girl clutching a towel around her.

Stella, I deduced.

"The bathroom's all yours, Becky," she announced, raking long white fingers through her newly washed hair. "I hope I haven't used up the all hot water again."

"Ah, never mind," Becky answered good-naturedly. "It's still a treat having an indoor bathroom." She picked up her wash bag and squeezed past Stella out of the room.

Stella turned a limpidly beautiful gaze on me. "Oh, hello," she said.

"This is Mary Seward," Helen told her. "She works on my shift at the sanatorium."

Stella flashed a perfect white smile, her teeth sparkling like pearls. "Pleased to meet you," she said. Holding her towel to her body with one hand, she held out the other to me.

"Pleased to meet you, Stella," I said as we shook hands. I held her in my gaze. Something about her made me uneasy.

"Mind if I borrow your robe, Helen?" Stella asked. Without waiting for an answer she turned, letting her towel slip to the floor as she unhooked the flowery kimono that hung on the door and then slipped into it.

I found myself gaping at Stella in surprise. The girl's brash confidence overwhelmed me. She was brazen, almost feline in her movements.

"How are you enjoying your work at the sanatorium?" I asked, wondering how such a free-spirited creature conformed to the quiet discipline of the wards.

"Well, it's good to be away from home," she answered, plopping down onto Helen's bed. She reached for a nail file that sat on Helen's nightstand and began flicking it idly across her nails. "I don't know about the sister on your shift, but ours is a stickler. She had me scrubbing bedpans till dawn. My nails are ruined." She held out five well-manicured fingers, and I felt instantly self-conscious about my own sore, bitten nails. I hid them furtively behind my back.

Helen rolled her eyes in mock exasperation. "Don't believe a word of it. Stella always exaggerates!" She grinned at Stella. "Becky told me that Sister is utterly charmed by you, just like everyone else."

A smile spread easily over Stella's full lips. "Well, Sister's a nice old bird really, once you get to know her."

Something in Stella's manner completely unsettled me. I knew that I didn't want to leave Father in her care—not even for a couple of hours. Perhaps with more time to get to know her, I might change my mind—but from what I'd seen, she did not seem the calm, patient sort of person I'd hoped to find.

I wondered if I should leave before Helen had the chance to ask Stella to sit with Father. I glanced apprehensively at my watch. It was getting late anyway; evening would be drawing in before long.

Yes, I decided, my anxiety flaring. I'll make my excuses and leave now.

But Helen must have sensed my growing agitation and assumed I was keen to broach the purpose of my visit. "Mary has a favor to ask," she began. "She's been asked to a party on the nineteenth, and she needs someone to sit with her father for—"

"He's very frail and needs constant care," I interrupted, secretly hoping that this might put Stella off.

"I'd sit with him myself," Helen went on. "But my Johnny's coming home that night. So I told Mary that if you and Becky were off duty that evening, maybe one of you would do it."

"Well, yes, we are off duty on the nineteenth," Stella answered at once. "And as far as *I'm* concerned, any chance to escape this place on an evening off is welcome. I'll do it, darling!"

I fought against the alarm that yawned within my chest.

Calm down, I told myself. If Helen trusts Stella, then why shouldn't I? After all, they shared the same digs.

"But I thought you'd agreed to see that Sam fellow on the nineteenth, Stella. . . ." Becky's soft lilt sounded hesitantly from the doorway. Her hair was now scraped back into an unbecoming bun and her glasses, slightly steamed up, made her look more owl-like than ever.

Stella frowned. "Oh yes . . ." She sighed irritably. "Goodness,

Becky, you know my calendar better than I do. You ought to get out more yourself."

Becky's cheeks grew pink at Stella's rather pointed comment.

"I just remembered you saying . . ." Becky said quietly.

"Sorry, Mary," Stella apologized. "I simply can't stand Sam up. He's such a darling. *And* rather rich," she added with a wink.

I felt the prickle of guilty relief. A small sigh escaped my lips.

"I could do it, though," Becky offered. She took off her spectacles to polish away the steam with one of the drooping cuffs on her dressing gown.

"Really?" Hope fluttered in my chest. Becky seemed far more suitable. She was clearly a good Catholic girl—and I felt a wave of sympathy for her, being away from home and family for the first time. A few hours of Father's company might be good for her too; despite his frailty, he still had his quick wit and warm manner. "Thank you, Becky," I said.

Becky perched her spectacles back on her nose, blinked, and then gave me a shy smile. "What time should I arrive?" she asked.

"Seven o'clock would be fine, if that's all right with you?" I replied.

"I'll be there," Becky promised.

I gave her directions—feeling well disposed toward the idea of leaving Father in someone else's care.

"That's settled, then," Helen said happily. "Would you like some tea before you go, Mary?"

I glanced again at my watch. It would be dark very soon. "That's kind, but I really must get home to Father," I excused myself.

"Very well, I'll show you out." Helen led me to the door, and I thanked her quickly, anxious to be gone. The sun was already low in the sky. As soon as she closed the front door, I turned and ran home.

Thank goodness it is not Stella who will be sitting with Father. Though it is no doubt my vexing paranoia that warns me against her, I could never have endured the party while feeling I might have left Father in unsafe hands.

But perhaps it is time to confront this paranoia, as Father insists, and to quash this nonsensical fear of the dark after all.

CHAPTER 9

EVENING TRIBUNE

10TH OCTOBER 1918

GRUESOME MURDER

A man's mutilated body has been found in Hitcham, Surrey. Farm laborer John Sands was discovered dead on Sunday morning by his workmate, Harry Pilling. Pilling found Sands's body tied to a cart wheel in the barn of Hatch Moor Farm. He was too shocked to comment.

Police say that Sands had been tortured before his death. His injuries were extensive. "By the time he was found, there was not a drop of blood left in him," Constable Richards told our reporter. "Though where it had gone, I don't know. Apart from the stains on his clothes, there was little on the floor and only a few splashes on the straw around the barn."

Sands had been gagged, explaining why no one had heard the sounds of what must have been an agonizing death. The police admit that they have no suspects yet, though they are questioning all inhabitants of the village.

The villagers themselves blame a passing vagrant for the horrendous crime. "No one from the village would have done such a thing," said veteran soldier Horace Earnshaw. "It reminds me of a field punishment some of the crueler officers used in the trenches. I reckon this murderer was someone come home from the front, shell-shocked. No one in their right mind could do such terrible things."

Journal of
Mary Seward

19TH OCTOBER 1918

Waiting for Becky to arrive this evening was an ordeal in itself. My heart thudded and sweat pricked my palms as I heard the clock strike seven. Just a quarter of an hour to go until Becky arrived. And then it would be time for me to leave the house and venture out into the night.

My stomach heaved with terror at the thought; I was

somehow certain that an awful fate must await me out there. I found myself utterly unable to sit still and paced up and down the parlor, every muscle in my body taut, like those of a soldier waiting to be sent into battle.

Who would believe I was only going out to dinner? I felt at once ridiculous and wretched.

"Settle down, my dear," Father advised from his chair beside the hearth. "You will be fine."

"It is so long since I have socialized," I replied weakly.

"Well, you are a charming young woman," Father assured me. "And tonight you look beautiful. There is even a little color back in your cheeks."

How could I tell him that the color was carefully applied rouge? I had spent an hour dressing, arranging my hair, and powdering my face to disguise the dark rings beneath my eyes. I just hoped the gown I had chosen—my best blue one, with the high lace collar and sparkling beads—would distract from my pallid face.

At exactly quarter past seven, the doorbell rang.

"Punctual too," Father commented approvingly.

My breath became shallow and gasping as my chest tightened with panic—but I would not let Father see. I hurried into the hall, my heart hammering fit to burst through my rib cage. I made myself suck in a lungful of air and then pulled open the door.

Becky was waiting on the step, this time dressed in a

plain brown coat and hat, with heavy-looking brogues on her feet. "Hello," she said cheerily. "Am I on time?"

"On the dot," I replied. "Please come in, Becky."

As she stepped past me, I couldn't help feeling a little uncomfortable in all my finery. I hoped she didn't think me vain. But I needn't have worried.

"You look as pretty as a picture," she told me as she unbuttoned her coat to reveal a plain blouse and skirt beneath.

I smiled my thanks and took her coat, conscious of my shaking hands, but Becky was already busy glancing around the hallway.

"I see I had no need to bring my holy water here," she commented with a smile as she noticed the crucifix hung on the far wall.

I nodded. "No boggarts or banshees in this house," I promised. "Only Father, and he's as gentle as a lamb."

"I'm so looking forward to meeting him." Becky beamed at me. "I hear he used to work at the sanatorium."

I nodded. "That's right," I confirmed. "And he's looking forward to meeting you too. He's housebound and doesn't see many new faces." I led her toward the parlor, pausing outside the door. "He's had his supper, but if you could make him some cocoa before he retires—"

"Mary . . . I'm sure your father will tell me if there's anything he needs," Becky told me gently.

I heard Father chuckle on the other side of the door. "My daughter does fuss over me rather too much," he agreed as we entered. "But it's only because she worries." He gave me an affectionate smile and then held out his hand to greet Becky.

Becky stepped forward and shook it. "It's an honor to meet you, Dr. Seward," she said.

"It's very kind of you to come and sit with an old man," Father replied. "I'm very keen that Mary has a chance to get out and about a bit more. This is the first time she's been out in months."

"Well, I'm sure it won't be the last," Becky said. "You do look so pretty, Mary." There seemed a thread of wistfulness in her voice as she repeated her compliment, and I silently resolved to see if I could help her make more of herself.

"Well, then, shouldn't you be going, Mary?" Father prompted me.

For a few brief minutes, I had been distracted from the ordeal that awaited me. At his words, my heart began to pound once more. "Yes . . ." I muttered. I bent and kissed his forehead. "See you in the morning."

Father smiled and nodded. "Enjoy yourself, my dear. I look forward to hearing all about it," he said. As I left the room, he turned to Becky, gesturing to the winged chair opposite his. "Come and make yourself comfortable, Becky," he invited.

KATE CARY

In the hallway I pulled on my coat, fumbling with the buttons, my fingers were so stiff with anxiety, and listened to the conversation beginning in the parlor.

"I was just telling Mary, I've heard you used to run the sanatorium before the war, Dr. Seward—when it was a private asylum," Becky was saying. "I'd love you to tell me about those days."

"Really?" Father said. I could hear the pleasure he took from Becky's interest. "Well, now," he said. "Let me see. Where to start . . ."

Once more feeling a wave of gratitude toward Becky, I quietly opened the front door. Father was in very capable hands.

I let myself out, glancing warily around the shadowed garden. If only it had been a summer evening, the sun still keeping the darkness at bay. Summoning up all my courage, I stepped out into the night.

Closing the garden gate behind me, I set off down the tree-lined lane, my gaze fixed firmly ahead. The Edwardses' home, Blanchard House, was scarcely half a mile away. It was impossible to justify ordering a cab for such a short distance. My hosts would have thought me mad.

I kept on reminding myself that I was in Purfleet, far from the horrors I had witnessed, and though every nerve in my body tingled with fear, I forced myself to keep walking, taking some comfort from the lighted windows beyond the gardens I passed. The rustling of the windblown trees did nothing to relieve the eerie emptiness of the lane, however. Was everyone safely inside but me?

At last, I turned a corner and saw the lights of Blanchard House ahead. My pace quickened. Then suddenly, something gleamed in the darkness up ahead of me. Two golden orbs. There was no mistaking them this time. A pair of eyes! Peering at me in the darkness!

I wanted to shriek, but my throat tightened in terror. My heart pounded until I thought it would crack open.

And then the creature sprang forward, landing deftly on the path in front of me.

I gasped—and then the creature mewed.

It was a cat, I realized. Just a cat. It had been staring down at me from a nearby garden wall. It twitched its tail at me before it scampered off.

Infuriated at my own ridiculous timidity, I marched on, more determined than ever not to be conquered by my overactive imagination. Still, I put my hand to my throat and fingered the comforting shape of my crucifix and its companion vial of holy water beneath my lace collar.

The garden path at Blanchard House was lit with paper lanterns that swung in the breeze, and bright light streamed from the windows. I saw people gathered beyond them and heard voices drifting from the house, talking and laughing. I hurried up the path and rang the doorbell with more than a little urgency, longing to be inside too, away from the darkness.

I'd written only a tentative reply to Jane's invitation, fearful of committing myself, saying I would attend the party only if Father were well enough. When Jane opened the door to me, she smiled with delight.

"Mary, you came after all!" she exclaimed.

"Yes," I breathed, feeling weak with relief as I crossed the threshold.

The interior behind her was awash with light and noise. Gentlemen in tuxedos and ladies in their best silks and taffetas milled around the room. Candles, placed seemingly everywhere, gave the place a cheerful yet sophisticated glow. At last, I felt a little rush of anticipation at meeting Jane's chatting, smiling guests. For a moment I felt part of the normal world, safe from my anxieties.

"Would you like to see Grace before I introduce you to some of our guests?" Jane offered as she took my coat.

I nodded eagerly.

Jane led me upstairs to Grace's nursery. "She's sleeping, but it won't disturb her if we peek," she whispered.

The cozy room was gently lit by a night-light. I approached the cot and gazed down at Grace, sleeping soundly, her sweet round face illuminated by the soft light. She looked an angel, with her halo of dark, silky curls, sweeping black lashes, and rosy cheeks. I reached down and

tucked her blanket around her warm little body, resting my
hand lightly on her chest so that I could feel her breathing.

"She'll sleep right through," Jane promised. "And I'll tell
her tomorrow you looked in on her. But for now, I want you
to concentrate on enjoying yourself, Mary. It doesn't matter
if you don't know anybody—I shall introduce you."

She led me out, leaving the nursery door ajar behind us,
and I followed her downstairs.

I felt a quiver of anxiety at the thought of meeting new
people, but I had come this far and was determined not to
falter now. Lifting my chin, I put on a friendly smile as Jane
led me into the crush of people gathered around the foot of
the staircase.

A handsome, fresh-faced young man intercepted me as I
tried to follow Jane through the crush. "And who might this
charming young lady be? Do introduce her, Janie," he
demanded as he seized my hand and kissed it.

His forwardness caught me off guard and I snatched my
fingers away, staring wordlessly at him.

"Bertie!" Jane reprimanded. "This is Miss Mary Seward.
Now do try and be more polite to our guests!" She smiled at
me apologetically. "This is my youngest brother, Robert
Gough," she said. "Don't let him alarm you. He's perfectly
harmless."

Robert feigned a hurt expression and then grinned. "Call
me Bertie," he invited. "Everyone does."

His cheery, open demeanor made me smile back, but I felt myself blushing and realized how unaccustomed I had become to socializing. "Pleased to meet you," I murmured.

Someone had caught Jane's eye. She was craning her neck and peering into the parlor. "That's Lord Xavier Bathory, standing by the window there," she told me, giving a little wave. "Andrew's new client. He's all by himself. I do hope he's not feeling out of place."

Through the open doorway, I spotted a slightly built, fair-haired man standing by the window, looking rather lost. There was something scholarly and old-fashioned about him, I thought; whether it was the tiny, wire-rimmed spectacles he wore or the rather drab suit he had chosen for the occasion, I wasn't quite sure.

"Lord Bathory approached Andrew on a friend's recommendation; he offered Andrew all of his family legal work, which has turned out to be quite substantial," Jane went on, her face shining with wifely pride. "Andrew can hardly believe his good fortune, being just a provincial lawyer. And Bathory's turned out to be a perfect darling. He's become quite a friend to us. It feels as though we've known him forever. . . ."

"Jane!" Andrew called across the room. He was pointing urgently toward the kitchen.

"Looks like an emergency for the hostess," Jane said with a sigh. She squeezed my hand reassuringly. "There's music and dancing in the drawing room. Bertie will look after you," she told me. "You will enjoy yourself, won't you, Mary?"

I forced a smile. "Of course I will," I promised.

Bertie looked pleased as Jane rushed off. "Miss Seward, do please dance with me," he urged. "You are quite the prettiest woman here, and it would do my reputation a world of good."

I smiled at his youthful flattery. "I might tread on your toes," I warned, not having danced in public for nearly two years.

"I don't think I'd notice if you did," Bertie answered, leading me into the large space in the middle of the drawing room, where the rug had been rolled back and the furniture pushed aside for the dancers.

As he energetically whisked me around the floor, Bertie told me he'd just gone up to Cambridge, and I realized he must be at least at least two years younger than my own nineteen. His being so young and Jane's brother helped me to relax a little, and I actually found myself quite enjoying the dance.

But then suddenly Bertie gasped and brought us to a sudden halt. I searched his ruddy face. His attention was drawn by someone or something among the spectators gathered around the dance floor.

"What is it?" I asked.

"Just act naturally," he said through an exaggerated smile.

"My Antonia's just arrived, and she's the jealous type. If she finds out I gave you the first dance—" He drew a finger across his throat, and I laughed at the exaggerated gesture. "Do you mind if I leave you for a moment?" he pleaded.

I followed his gaze and saw a pretty dark-haired girl standing at the edge of the dance floor. She was looking nervously around the room and could have been no more than sixteen. "I think you should go to her right away," I told him. "She looks positively lost. And besides, your sister would never forgive me if I were the cause of—" I mimicked his throat-cutting gesture.

Bertie exhaled. "I knew you'd understand." He turned and tapped a tall, dark-haired man on the shoulder. "Giles, would you look after Miss Seward for me?"

The dark-haired man turned, gave me an appraising look, and then smiled. I felt a tremor of anxiety; there was something slightly unsavory in his gaze.

"It would be a pleasure, Bertie," he said, holding out a hand to me. "Giles Maitland." He introduced himself with a little bow.

Reluctantly I let him lead me back among the dancers, my disconcertment rising at the tight grip he kept on my hand.

"I spotted you earlier," he murmured in my ear as he held me, too closely, against him. "Silly little Bertie for passing you on."

I pulled away from the hold he had on me and kept him at arm's length as we danced. My propriety seemed to amuse him.

"I'm curious as to how our paths have not crossed before tonight," he commented.

"I don't go out much," I answered coolly. "My father's health isn't good, and I don't like to leave him."

"Ah," he responded. "A dutiful daughter. How charming."

As soon as the music ended, I felt a rush of relief. The dancing had made me hot, and Mr. Maitland's overly tight grip had awoken a feeling of claustrophobia in me. I longed for cool, fresh air. "Thank you for the dance," I said politely as I pulled my hands free from his, "but I should like to take some air now."

The French windows that led out onto the wide, flag-stoned terrace were open. I could see that the terrace was lit with lanterns, and, feeling I should be safe enough out there, I made my way to the door.

The cool evening air bathed me as I stepped out. I crossed over to the terrace edge to lean on its cold stone balustrade. It was a relief to be out of the crowded room, but as I looked out upon the dark garden beyond, I felt my familiar anxiety begin to stir.

"It's a beautiful evening, isn't it?"

I spun around to see that Giles Maitland had followed me out. My anxiety grew. "It is lovely," I agreed, not meeting his gaze. "However, I was about to go back inside." I turned to leave—but Mr. Maitland, not to be shaken so easily, placed a hand on my arm to stay me. My heart began to race a little; I was intimidated by his forwardness.

"Surely you don't have to leave just yet," he said. "It's a rare treat to find such an attractive woman out here in the country."

Was he ignoring my lack of interest on purpose? "I'm sorry," I replied. "The air is a little chilly out here. I want to go in." I pulled away from his grasp—but as I turned, a sudden loud fluttering rose from a tree beside the terrace. I caught my breath as the dark, web-winged shape of a bat loomed up into the moonlight.

The creature swooped beneath the string of lanterns edging the terrace and dove across the balustrade so close to me I felt the air from its wings on my cheek. Speechless terror ripped through me and I lurched backward—falling against Mr. Maitland.

I found myself gripped in his tight embrace. "Ah, changed your mind, have you?" he murmured in a knowing tone that made me shudder. He spun me around to face him. "That's more like it."

"Let go of me!" I gasped, pushing against his chest.

But he just laughed and held me tighter. "I like a woman with spirit. I believe this will be a kiss worth fighting for. . . ."

I recoiled in horror as he lowered his mouth toward mine.

"Maitland!" A man's voice spoke from the doorway. "It

should be clear—even to you—that the lady does not welcome your attentions."

Taken by surprise, my captor loosened his grip. I immediately pulled myself free and, panting with relief, turned to identify my savior.

Standing in the doorway was the man Jane had pointed out earlier. Andrew's employer, Lord Bathory.

The two men gazed at each other for a long moment—and then Mr. Maitland backed away. "Provincials," he muttered. With an angry snort, he strode back into the house.

"I have never been able to stand that man," Lord Bathory commented after Maitland had gone. "I've known him since Eton, and he's always been a bully."

"Th-thank you," I stuttered, my voice trembling.

"You look shaken," Lord Bathory noted, concern in his voice. "May I fetch you some refreshment? A sherbet, perhaps? Sweetness, I believe, is good for shock."

I shook my head, taking deep breaths to calm my still-pounding heart. "Thank you, but I think I'd rather go home," I replied.

"Oh no." Lord Bathory looked at me, his gray eyes earnest behind his spectacles. "Do not let a cad like Maitland frighten you away," he said. "I'm sure our hosts would be disappointed if you left so soon." He tipped his head to one side. "And that buffoon, Maitland, would take it as a victory if you fled."

His words struck the right note in me. Of course I shouldn't let a bully like Mr. Maitland drive me from the party, and it would be too bad of me to disappoint dear Jane. "You are right," I agreed, my voice a little stronger now.

Lord Bathory smiled. "Good," he said. And then he started. "What am I thinking?" he went on. "Do please forgive my lack of manners. I have not yet introduced myself. Lord Xavier Bathory." He bowed slightly and held out his hand.

With a smile, I took it. "I know who you are," I confessed. "Jane told me. I'm Mary Seward."

"Mary Seward . . ." Lord Bathory pondered, as if trying to remember something. "Ah—I have it!" he said. "Little Grace's savior! How delightful to meet you."

I felt my cheeks flush again; I was quite disconcerted by the way Lord Bathory was now gazing at me with such frank admiration. "N-not exactly a savior," I stammered. "I only brought her back from Europe. It is Andrew and Jane who have given her a loving home."

Lord Bathory lowered his pale lashes. "I seem to have embarrassed you," he said. "I am so sorry. Will you forgive me?"

"Of course," I replied, grateful for his sensitivity.

Looking relieved, Lord Bathory went on. "I had not expected to find anyone else hiding out here on such a chilly night," he admitted. "I would hate dear Jane to know how ill at ease I feel among such a lively crowd. She is a hostess of great kindness and consideration."

I smiled guiltily at him. "I came out here to hide too," I said. "Your secret is safe with me. But perhaps we should go back in now before we are missed."

Lord Bathory nodded. "Perhaps if we face the throng together, it won't seem so daunting."

"Perhaps," I responded, a good measure of doubt in my voice.

Side by side, we reentered the drawing room. A roar went up from the crowd as the band struck up one of the latest tunes from America.

"I think something a little stronger than a sherbet may be required," Bathory whispered, staring ahead in dismay.

"A glass of wine at least," I answered, almost smiling.

It was strange. Though I'd never met Lord Bathory before, it felt as though we were co-conspirators, and I found myself surprisingly at ease in his company.

"Do you think you might survive here alone while I brave the throng and fetch us each one?" he asked.

I nodded, welcoming his gentle humor. I found myself tapping my foot in time to the music, and when he returned with our glasses, we fell into easy conversation until dinner was served—a hot buffet followed by a delicious choice of puddings and desserts.

"Ah, I see you two have already introduced yourselves,"

Jane observed, clearly delighted as she passed by carrying another huge fruit trifle to the table.

After we had eaten, Lord Bathory and I moved to the quietness of the parlor and took chairs beside the fire to continue our tête-à-tête.

The subject of literature came up.

"I fear you'll find me rather dry on that topic," Lord Bathory told me apologetically. "I would rather grow dusty among the classics. Modern writers seem so sure they have the answers—and yet anyone who has read Thucydides will know we are still making the same mistakes; one has only to look at the war."

"You would like my father," I commented. "He also is well read in the classics—though I'm afraid I never got much past Virgil."

"There is little wrong with that—Virgil is a marvelous writer!" Lord Bathory's eyes shone with enthusiasm. He began to quote a passage I'd learned as a girl and still remembered. "'It is easy to go down into Hell; night and day, the gates of dark Death stand wide. . . .'"

"'But to climb back again, to retrace one's steps to the upper air—there's the rub, the task.'" I completed the quote for him.

Lord Bathory stared at me in surprise.

"You did not expect such education in a woman?" I teased him.

"Certainly not in Purfleet," he answered, suppressing a smile, which his eyes betrayed.

I suddenly realized that for the first time in a very long while, I felt truly at ease. If only for that reason, leaving Lord Bathory's pleasant company would be something of a cause for regret. As I remembered the journey home ahead of me, my heart grew heavy again and the unwelcome pounding in my chest returned. "I really must think about making my way home," I said quietly. "I have someone sitting with my invalid father; I should not keep her out too late."

Lord Bathory nodded. "I understand. Shall I call for your carriage?" he offered as we both stood.

I shook my head. "I walked here; I live only a few minutes away," I explained.

"Then you must use my carriage," Lord Bathory insisted. "It's frosty out there now, and the lanes may be slippery underfoot. I have business to discuss with Andrew before I leave, so I'll be staying for some time."

"You are kind, but I couldn't," I protested.

"Please take my carriage," Lord Bathory gently insisted. "My driver will be back long before I need it."

I smiled at up him gratefully. "Thank you!" I breathed, relief washing over me like a tidal wave. I grasped Lord Bathory's hand and shook it warmly. "You have no idea how you have put me at ease."

At the touch of my hand, Bathory looked alarmed. He

took a step backward. "I—I am glad to be of service," he stammered, looking at his shoes.

How foolish of me. I had only known Bathory for an hour or two. It was wrong of me to have been so forward with him.

"I'm so sorry," I apologized at once, hot with embarrassment as I quickly let go of his hand. "It must be the wine. . . ."

He glanced up at me. "No. It is I who should apologize," he said carefully. "As we have just seen, my shyness can sometimes be an impediment to politeness." He smiled ruefully, and I felt my embarrassment evaporate. His self-awareness touched me.

"Do please forgive me if I gave the impression of feeling anything but pleasure at our meeting, Miss Seward," he went on. "It has been delightful, and I hope to have the privilege of your company again one day."

I smiled my forgiveness, and Lord Bathory gave a relieved little nod.

"I'll call for my carriage, then," he said, making for the hall, "and ask Jane to fetch your coat."

Jane accompanied me to the front door while Bathory advised his driver where he should drop me. His carriage was a stately brougham with a gray mare fidgeting in its harness.

"I suppose I ought to get one of these newfangled motor carriages," Lord Bathory commented conversationally as he handed me into the secure comfort of the brougham. "But I can't imagine the sound of an engine can ever be as beautiful as that of hooves."

I nodded my thanks to him and called goodbye to Jane. They both waved as the driver closed the door. I fell back onto the soft leather seat and let the gentle rocking of the brougham lull me into tranquility.

The night, it seemed, had been a success.

LATER

Arriving home, I found Becky alone in the parlor, reading the newspaper.

"Oh, it is you!" she said with a smile as I walked in. "I thought I heard a carriage pull up outside." She put down the paper and stood, pushing her spectacles back up her nose with one finger.

"How was Father?" I asked anxiously.

"Oh, we had a lovely chat," Becky reported. "He is such an interesting man, your father! And then I made him some cocoa and helped him up the stairs to bed. I think he quite enjoyed the company. I certainly did." She beamed.

I smiled back. She really was sweet. "Thank you so much, Becky," I replied. "Will you be safe getting home?"

"To be sure," Becky replied. "I'm just a few strides away." She took her coat and headed for the door.

"Thanks again, Becky," I said as she took her leave. She crossed herself with a small vial of holy water and then disappeared through the garden gate. I blew out the lamp and bolted the door before going straight upstairs to bed.

The relief of arriving safely home and of finding Father also safe and well has brought with it a deep exhaustion— but I felt it important to record the events of this evening. It has been such a night. For the first time in almost two years, I overcame my fears enough to venture out into the dark. In Becky, Father and I seem to have hit upon the ideal companion for him. And thanks to Lord Bathory, my evening out became a pleasure instead of an ordeal. No small thing! Father will be so pleased when I tell him in the morning.

Perhaps the darkness and terror I felt have passed at last!

CHAPTER 10

*Note from Lord Xavier Bathory
to Miss Mary Seward*

THE ROYAL HOTEL
PURFLEET
23RD OCTOBER 1918

Dear Miss Seward,

I wanted to send flowers days ago but worried I might seem over-solicitous. Now I fear I have left it too late and you will think me offhand. But I send them today, no matter what—your agreeable company spurring my determination to overcome my vexing shyness. I hope you will accept the bouquet in gratitude for making my evening at Blanchard House such a pleasant and memorable one.

While I am being so bold, might I ask if you would consider dining with me one evening at my hotel? I will quite understand if you would rather not—but if you would care to, I promise not to bore you with too much Thucydides. . . .

Yours sincerely,
Xavier Bathory

Journal of
Mary Seward

23RD OCTOBER 1918

I have just received flowers from Lord Bathory—an exquisite bouquet! The parlor already smells heavenly with the scent. What is more, Lord Bathory's note contains an invitation to dine with him.

I don't know what to feel about the proposition. I am sure I would enjoy another evening in his company, though that would, of course, mean braving the night again. . . .

However, if Lord Bathory has found it within himself to stand up to his shyness and invite me, then shouldn't I at least attempt to do him the service of matching that courage with an acceptance?

I made a few blooms from Lord Bathory's bouquet into a posy for Father's study and took it in to him—as much to gain his opinion on Lord Bathory's invitation as to brighten his day.

He was seated on the sofa, struggling to fold his morning newspaper. The great broadsheet seemed to have got the better of him, and I fear I heard an oath as he flapped it first this way, then the other.

I placed the small vase of flowers on his desk, which he rarely uses anymore, and then offered to take the paper from him and fold it back to the page he required.

Reluctantly he handed it over. "I pray I have not grown too weak to manage the *Times*," he huffed. "I have few enough pleasures left."

I bent down and kissed his frowning brow, pained to hear him so distressed.

"You are a good daughter," he told me, looking mollified. Then he caught sight of the flowers. "Thank you, my dear, very thoughtful of you. And such fine blooms for so late in the year," he commented.

"A gentleman sent them to me," I told him.

"A gentleman?" Father raised an eyebrow.

I nodded. "One I met at the Edwardses' party."

"Why did you not mention him earlier?" Father asked curiously.

I gave a little shrug. "We chatted, but I thought it only a casual meeting," I explained. "I did not expect to hear from him again . . . but he's invited me to join him for dinner."

Father's expression changed to one of delight mixed with caution. "Does he seem . . . trustworthy, Mary?" he asked.

I fell silent, pondering. Trustworthy? I had trusted John— only to watch him transform into a treacherous fiend. Lord Bathory did not have the youthful bravado of the John I had fallen in love with—nor the calculating charm and good looks of the evil Quincey Harker. Despite his aristocratic background, Lord Bathory was studious and reserved—his mind surely too full of philosophy and his heart too beset by timidity to be capable of deception? Deception required a determined and fierce single-mindedness. "Yes, Father, I think Lord Bathory is trustworthy," I answered quietly.

"Bathory? Lord Xavier Bathory?" Father queried, his tone one of surprise.

"You know him?" I asked, surprised now myself.

"I know of him," Father replied. He tapped the *Times* with a finger. "I have read some of the speeches he has given in Parliament. He must have a keen sense of duty, for they say he battles a natural shyness when standing to speak before his peers. But from what I've read, I'm glad he does. He seems like a well-read and levelheaded young man, which is just what this government needs."

"Then you think I should accept his invitation?" I asked.

It was Father's turn to fall silent, concern shadowing his eyes. "You know I cannot help but worry about you, Mary," he said eventually. "I nearly lost you once. But it is my dearest wish to see you find happiness with a good man. I cannot bear to think you might grow old alone. So yes, I think you should accept his invitation."

"Father, Lord Bathory did not mean his invitation as any sort of proposal, I'm sure," I told him. A smile tickled my lips at the thought of Lord Bathory's discomposure at the idea. "But I doubt if I will meet a man safer than he."

And so, with Father's approval, I have written my acceptance note and shall hire a carriage for the journey there and back.

ESSEX FARMER'S WEEKLY

2ND NOVEMBER 1918

SLAUGHTERED SHEEP

REWARD OFFERED

Purfleet farmer Bill Watts is prepared to pay a ten-guinea reward to anyone who can help him catch the creature responsible for killing four of his sheep. Bite marks on the animals' necks suggest the culprit is a large hound.

"I've not seen killings like this before," Watts

commented. "It seems the varmint kills just for the sport of it. It don't savage nothing but the neck and takes no meat. If I catch the villain, I shall shoot it from here to kingdom come, and I'll give ten guineas to anyone who catches it afore me!"

Journal of
Quincey Harker

CARFAX HALL
PURFLEET
3RD NOVEMBER 1918

It is strange to be back in this place.

Two years ago, I was here as Lily's guest and suitor—and the very air felt alive with her sweet, trusting presence. Now these rooms feel dead, everywhere dulled by absence and dust.

No one has been within these walls since I hurried Lily away on our elopement to Transylvania, Antanasia fussing over our luggage, urging us to be gone, unconcerned about what we left behind. The dusty floors are now lined with shafts of sunlight, which slice their way like knives through the gaps between the shutters. Plants slump, dried up and dead in their pots. The kitchen lies filthy, ruined by mice and rats that feasted on the food we left behind and scuttle still among the flour sacks and putrid remains of the pantry.

Nothing here has changed—and yet everything has. It is a gloomy house. I imagine it always was, except for the short time Lily graced its chambers. As I wander through its hallways, I half expect to hear her gentle voice calling from the stairs, searching me out as she used to, craving the comfort of my embrace. But I shall not dwell on such memories.

My suffering in the catacombs—surviving on the humblest of prey—has sharpened my hunger. It twists my belly and tortures my soul. But I am near my goal now: I can sense Mary Seward's proximity as a wolf scents its prey.

I shall call on her soon.

Chapter 11

Journal of Mary Seward

I have just returned from my dinner with Lord Bathory—though he insists I now call him just Bathory, as his other friends do.

I had never had reason to visit the Royal Hotel before but, of course, had passed it many times, having grown up in Purfleet. I'd always been impressed by the hotel's imposing Victorian facade, its steeply pitched gables and sweeping lawns.

It wasn't easy, venturing out into the night again, despite the protection of the covered carriage. My heart pounded as we traveled through the darkened lanes. I peered fretfully out of the carriage window, searching the shadows; somehow, not looking was even more frightening. But knowing Bathory awaited me, I found the strength to bear the anxiety

that seared my veins. I hoped I'd find him as convivial as
when last we met.

I hurried from the brougham into the welcoming light of
the Royal Hotel's lobby and found myself awed by its opulence. My nose was immediately filled with the heady scent
coming from a spectacular display of hothouse lilies positioned to the side of the sweeping central staircase. I made
my way, a little self-consciously, toward the reception desk,
my tread sinking into the deep-piled carpet. I felt my rather
plain dress must look dowdy amid such elegance.

But the immaculately dressed man behind the desk
smiled warmly as I approached, and as soon as I told him my
name, he quickly ushered me into the dining room and led
me toward an empty table.

"I will call Lord Bathory's room and tell him you have
arrived," he informed me, taking my coat as I slipped it from
my shoulders. He draped it over his arm and pulled out a
chair so that I might seat myself. The snow-white tablecloth
seemed to whisper as it brushed against the pale green silk of
my dress. My nose was filled with another heavenly scent—
of roses this time, decorating the center of the table.

As the man withdrew, I gazed around the room. It was lit
by new electric lamps hanging from the ceilings and fixed to
the walls, the vivid light glittering on the crystal glasses and
silverware that graced the tables. I felt I had entered the very
lap of luxury.

"Would you care for a drink, miss, while you are waiting?"

Starting at the unexpected voice, I turned to see that a waiter had appeared beside me, like a genie from a lamp. "Just a glass of water, please," I replied, relieved that my answer had come out with some degree of self-assurance. "And would you ask for Lord Bathory's carriage to be ready for me at ten?"

"Certainly, miss."

I caught sight of Bathory hurrying into the room just then, looking a little flustered. He was still straightening his tie as he headed toward the table, his gray eyes full of apology.

"Open some champagne, Simkins," he said to the waiter, his voice breathless.

The waiter glanced at me. "Will you still require water, miss?" he asked pleasantly.

I saw Bathory's face cloud with uncertainty on hearing this.

"Oh no, champagne would be lovely!" I quickly replied, secretly a little thrilled.

Looking relieved, Bathory seated himself opposite me, smoothing his fair hair hurriedly with his hand. "Do forgive me for not being here to greet you," he apologized. "I found myself lost in a book I picked up in London this morning and forgot the time."

"I've been here no more than a minute or two," I assured him.

124

Simkins returned with the champagne then. He filled our glasses and, with a respectful nod, silently glided away again.

Bathory picked up his champagne flute. "Let's make a toast," he said. "To another pleasant evening in excellent company."

I picked up my own glass and touched it against his. I was surprised to discover that I found Bathory to be somewhat more handsome than I remembered—despite his slightly disheveled appearance! But more importantly, I was relieved to feel the same comfort in his company as before.

"How was your journey?" he asked.

"It was quite comfortable, though I do not like to travel in the dark," I confessed. It seemed right to be honest.

"You should have said!" Bathory exclaimed. He snatched the spectacles from his nose, and I saw his gray eyes were filled with concern. "We might have had lunch together instead of dinner."

"No, no," I replied. "It is a ridiculous fear of mine, and I am determined to overcome it."

"Then I'm sure you will," Bathory replied kindly. "Nevertheless, would you like me to travel back with you later?"

"No, thank you," I answered, touched by his concern. "I won't conquer this fear if I am mollycoddled."

Bathory smiled. "Bravo, Miss Seward," he exclaimed. "If only I had half as much conviction, I should fashion myself into someone else entirely."

He picked up one of the two menus that had been left at the side of the table for us and handed it to me. "Now, what shall we eat?" he asked, picking up the other.

A wave of gratitude swelled in me as I watched him run his finger down the list of dishes. What an easy person he was to know.

The waiter returned to our table.

"Ah, Simkins," Bathory greeted him. "Perfect timing—I am ravenous."

"I'm pleased to see you have a guest tonight, my lord," Simkins said. He looked at me and confided, "Most nights his lordship's only companion is a book."

"I shall do my best to rival such companionship," I vowed, smiling.

"I'm sure you shall, miss," answered Simkins, his eyes twinkling. "Are you ready to order?"

I had not yet looked at my menu, but I knew that I would choose fish. The bloody texture of meat had held no appeal for me since my return from Transylvania. "What fish would you recommend?" I asked Simkins.

"We have some excellent John Dory, Miss Seward," Simkins answered at once. "Or there is lobster, should you prefer."

"John Dory sounds perfect," I told him.

He nodded and turned to Bathory. "And you, my lord?"

"John Dory too," Bathory replied.

"Very good, sir." Simkins lifted our menus and carried them away.

Bathory leaned toward me over the table, "So, Mary Seward," he said. "I am keen to hear more about you—especially of how a girl from Purfleet came to be able to quote Virgil!" he added with a smile.

I hesitated, unsure of how to begin. "Well . . ." I started. "I'm the only child of a provincial doctor who taught me to have an appreciation for each of his many enthusiasms." I touched one of the velvety red blooms in the center of the table. "I am unused to glamorous surroundings such as these, though we have a comfortable home. Until he retired due to ill health, just before the war started, my father ran the local sanatorium in Purfleet."

"And your mother?" Bathory asked.

"Mother was a nurse until she married Father," I replied. "And then she devoted her time to me and the household. She died seven years ago."

"I'm sorry to hear that," Bathory said sympathetically. "You are following in her footsteps?" he asked. "With the nursing, I mean."

"I am only a VAD nurse," I explained hurriedly. "I have little formal training. But when the war started, I felt I must do something."

"When the war is over—what are your plans then?" Bathory queried.

I gave a shrug. "I had dreamed of going to university to study medicine like Father," I confided. "He ensured that I received a good education in the hope that I would gain a place in one of the new women's colleges at Oxford. But then the war came . . . and so much has happened since it began, I feel utterly changed," I told him honestly.

"The war cannot last much longer," Bathory predicted. "There are tanks on the battlefield now—they must settle the thing one way or another. No more of this slow, entrenched carnage."

"I pray you are right," I breathed, thinking of the seemingly endless stream of soldiers still arriving at the sanatorium, their flesh ripped apart by shell fire, their skin and lungs burned by mustard gas.

"Perhaps when the war really is over, you might feel able to return to your dreams of university and a career," Bathory pressed.

"You approve of women having professions?" I asked.

"To the highest degree!" Bathory exclaimed. "The world loses much by favoring only half its population." His tone was earnest. "And I do not believe that such ambition need rule out marriage, either."

Caught off guard by the unexpected mention of marriage, the scar on my heart left by John seemed to burn in my chest.

Bathory must have seen the distress in my face. "Oh, dear," he said quietly. "Have I touched on a delicate subject?"

I lowered my gaze uncomfortably. "I was engaged to be married once," I confessed. "But my fiancé turned out to be . . . different . . . than I thought he was."

My voice trailed away as painful memories flooded my mind. I had no wish to pursue this subject further and so changed it with a question of my own. "What was the book that made you late for dinner?" I asked.

Bathory smiled. "A volume about the radiotelegraph," he answered. "It is a fascinating read. I find myself intrigued by the whole invention. I am keen to know how electricity can possibly convey a human voice. . . ."

Our conversation tumbled on, dinner quickly passing. And then we were sipping coffee. Bathory's keen mind might have intimidated me were it not for the gentleness and diplomacy with which he offered his arguments. I could see why he had begun to make his mark in Parliament and could imagine him going far, in years to come, so long as his shyness did not hinder him.

Only when Simkins approached our table and solicitously informed me that the carriage was waiting outside did I realize how much time had passed.

"Already?" Bathory asked, regret clear in his voice.

He escorted me to the entrance, helping me with my coat when Simkins brought it over. Frost had gathered on the grass and I pulled my coat around me, shivering as much at the cold as at the darkness.

"It will be warmer in the brougham," Bathory promised, opening the door of the cab. He held out a hand to help me inside. It felt reassuringly strong.

Bathory closed the carriage door, and I drew down its window and leaned out to him. "Thank you for a lovely dinner. I've enjoyed this evening very much," I told him honestly.

"Then we might do it again?" Bathory asked tentatively.

I nodded. "I'd like that."

Looking pleased, he stepped back and lifted a hand in farewell as the carriage pulled away.

A surge of elation lifted me. In Bathory's company, I felt safe. Almost normal. Suddenly it seemed possible that I might rejoin the bright, busy world I had known before. Buoyed by happiness, I did not feel the need to peer from the carriage window or wonder what might be lurking beyond.

But before we reached the hotel gate, the carriage screeched to a halt, the horse whinnying in alarm. And then a wild hammering began on the carriage window beside me. Someone was pounding it with a fist. My heart lurched into panic. "What is wrong?" I called out to the driver, too frozen with fear to pull up the blind and see who knocked so fiercely.

Before he could answer, a woman's voice sounded out. "Mary? Is it you in there?"

I raised the blind to peer out of the window.

Stella stared in at me. "Oh, thank goodness!" she cried.

I pulled down the window to hear her better. "Stella? What are you doing here?"

"I thought it was you I saw in the hotel lobby," she told me, her voice breathless. "I was supposed to meet Sam here, outside the hotel, but he's stood me up—can you believe it!"

Sympathy came instinctively to me at hearing her plight. "Oh, you poor thing," I said.

"So would you mind dropping me home on your way?" she asked. "I've no money for a cab, and these shoes are killing me!"

Her request reawakened caution in me. I remembered my first wary impression of this girl—her brazenness—her feline movements. The thought now of sharing a carriage with her filled me with trepidation.

A thought came unbidden. *You have not seen her in daylight. Perhaps she is one of them. . . .*

"Come on, Mary—open the door!" Stella seemed surprised at my hesitation. "It's cold out here!"

I considered a moment. Was I being unreasonable? I had no evidence that Stella was anything other than mortal. Could I really abandon her here just to satisfy my own paranoia? I grasped my crucifix and holy water tightly to reassure myself of their presence. Then I forced a smile and opened the carriage door.

Stella climbed in and sat beside me. "Thanks, Mary,

you're a treasure!" she exclaimed, turning to smile at me. Her white teeth seemed to gleam. Even here, in the dim interior of the carriage, she smelled of the cold night air.

I shuddered and slid my fingers between the buttons of my collar to finger the vial concealed behind.

"Fancy Sam standing *me* up like that! The *nerve*!" Stella sank back into her seat and then gave me a conspiratorial smile. "I suspect he may be married, you know. Maybe his wife found out. . . ."

I watched her closely, searching her face and her demeanor for any sign that she might be possessed of vampiric qualities. But her teeth showed no sharpness, her eyes no hint of red—and her pallor, I saw now, was simply face powder. I let my fingers fall from my throat. I'd let my anxiety get the better of me once more. Gradually my mind let go of its feverish whirl of doubt.

"You can drop me here." Stella's abrupt announcement a minute or so later took me by surprise.

"But where are you going?" I asked, startled. "We're still a distance from your house."

"I'm not going straight home," Stella announced. She banged on the carriage roof to signal to the driver to stop, and as the carriage pulled to a halt, she opened the door and jumped easily down.

"But—wait," I cautioned her. "It is late. Are you not afraid, walking on your own at this hour?"

Stella pulled her coat tight around her. "Mary, I've just been stood up, but I'll be damned before I waste a precious night off." She pointed to a nearby tavern. "If I slip into the tavern for a bit, I might find some *other* attention." Her words dripped with meaning.

"But—"

She winked. "Trust me. The most dangerous thing in Purfleet tonight—is yours truly." She slammed the coach door shut. "Thanks for the lift! You're an angel!" she called up to me, and then she turned and walked away.

I called to the driver to move on.

Now that she was gone, I felt foolish to have been so distrustful. Stella was just an exuberant girl. And I'd be well served to take a page from her book. I decided I would not let those few tremulous moments cloud what had been a perfect evening. I had ventured out without harm, and I should feel pleased. I would cap my evening with one final triumph. "You may leave me at the corner," I called up to the driver, taking Stella's cue as we neared my house.

The carriage dropped me off as I'd requested and rumbled away. I found myself alone in the empty lane. The great night sky yawned above me. My old anxiety sparked—but I kept it in check. I could see my garden gate in the moonlight and fought the urge to hasten toward it. Instead I compelled myself to walk slowly, urging my tightening muscles to relax, struggling to keep my breathing even. The soft breeze rattled the last leaves clinging to the branches above me, but I forced myself not to look up. Finally I let myself through the garden gate, a sense of triumph surging in my breast.

As I made my way up the garden path to the front door, a fox yowled in the distance, the unearthly noise finally unsettling my nerves. Quickly I fumbled for the key in my bag, the familiar panic beginning to take hold of me. The back of my neck grew hot with a prickling sensation—the feeling of being watched.

And not just a feeling. This time, it seemed like utter certainty. Who was there, hiding out in the darkness?

Another howl, closer this time.

My heart lurched. I hastily scanned the shadowy garden behind me but could see no movement.

I found the front door key and jammed it into the lock. I pushed open the door and then slammed it behind me.

There was a figure in the shadows at the foot of the stairs. I clutched my throat, gasping out loud. Then I realized it was Becky and laughed in relief.

"Sorry if I startled you." Becky grinned. "I've just come down from checking on your father."

"Is everything all right?" I asked anxiously.

Becky hesitated. "Well, I hate to even mention it, but he seemed a tad listless this evening," she informed me with a little frown. "I suggested he have an early night and helped him to bed. He is sleeping well now. So I think he was simply tired."

"I shall go and see to him," I said, pulling off my coat and making for the staircase.

Becky gently touched my arm and drew me back. "I checked on him not a moment ago, Mary," she said. "He's sleeping peacefully. Best not disturb him, eh? Rest will do him more good than anything. He'll be fine by the morning, I'm sure."

I took my foot off the bottom step with a sigh. Becky was right. I was over-reacting.

She took my coat from me and hung it up. "Shall I make us some tea?" she offered. "It will warm you up. It must have been chilly out there."

I nodded. "Tea would be lovely," I replied gratefully.

Becky patted my arm. "Good," she said. "You go and warm yourself in front of the parlor fire and I'll put the kettle on."

I did as she suggested and soon felt a little calmer as I reflected on the progress I had made that evening. Though I had not completely conquered my fears, I felt well on the way.

Before long, Becky entered carrying the tea tray.

"There was frost as I returned," I told her as she filled two cups. "You will be careful not to slip on your way home?"

"It's sweet of you to think of it, Mary, but my shoes are

sturdy," Becky assured me with a smile. She handed me a cup and settled back on the sofa.

"Do you really think Father is just tired?" I fretted. "He's been so ill in the past."

"Your father might not be in the best of health," Becky said seriously, "but he still has a lot of fight left in him. He would not give in easily to my insistence he go to bed. He wanted to wait up for you to hear about your evening with Lord Bathory!"

I stared at her gratefully. "Becky, you are such a comfort."

She clicked her tongue dismissively at the compliment and abruptly twisted the subject back around to my evening. "Your father's not the only one who's eager to hear how your evening went," she said, a gleam in her eye.

And so I told her and found it a pleasure to do so. Since Lily died, I have sorely missed a friend to whom I could confide in matters of the heart. I told Becky every detail of the evening.

"Oh, how exciting!" she exclaimed, her eyes wide behind her spectacles when I told her that Bathory had asked to see me again. "Imagine! You are being courted by a lord!"

I smiled and nodded. I hadn't the heart to spoil her romantic notions by telling her that it was Bathory's intelligence and sensitivity that most attracted me. And most importantly, that he somehow made me feel safe.

Despite Becky's reassurances, I couldn't stop myself from

hurrying up the stairs to check on Father after she had left.
As quietly as I could, I let myself into his room.

He was indeed sleeping, but I was alarmed to see how very pale he looked—and his breathing was shallow. Panic shot through me as I held his wrist—the pulse felt quite faint. This was surely more than just fatigue? The pallor, the shallow breathing . . . the symptoms Father had were indicative of a vampire bite.

My anxieties awoken again; they possessed me now. I hastily pulled back the collar of Father's nightshirt to check for bite marks.

There was no sign of such harm.

I felt myself calming again, common sense beginning to return.

Of course there were no bites! There had been no sign at all that evil had infested the parish. I had faced the night, and nothing had threatened me except my own paranoid suspicions.

And so I have retired to bed. I really must try not to indulge these panics of mine. It does no one any good—least of all Father.

If he appears no better in the morning, I shall call in the doctor to him.

CHAPTER 12

Journal of
Quincey Harker

CARFAX HALL
PURFLEET
4TH NOVEMBER 1918

Tonight I went again to Mary Seward's house.

Her father's bedroom was still illuminated—I flitted up to the roof to where I could lean over and peer in through a chink in the heavy curtains

Miss Seward was there, tending to her father.

"Mary, dear?" the old man murmured. "It is stuffy in here again. Open the window; there's a dear girl."

"It's frosty out, Father," Miss Seward protested.

"Just a crack will be enough," her father pleaded.

I heard the wooden creak of the frame as Miss Seward pulled up the sash just an inch.

The fragrance of warm flesh that seeped out into the cold

night air sent me momentarily dizzy from hunger and I almost lost my grip. I dragged myself across the tiles, away from the window, and lay there—waiting.

"Good night, Father. Sleep well," I heard Miss Seward say. The light was extinguished, and I heard the door close as she left her father alone.

I cannot wait much longer.

Journal of
Mary Seward

9TH NOVEMBER 1918

Father has grown worse, I fear! After examining him this morning, Dr. Jamieson asked to speak with me in the parlor.

My heart hammering in dread of what he might report, I showed him in, drawing back the curtains to let in the weak sunshine. We sat stiffly facing each other on either side of the hearth.

"Mary, I confess I am still at a loss as to what exactly ails your father," Dr. Jamieson began gravely.

"My God. Is there really nothing you can think of that might help him?" I begged. "Surely there must be something in this day and age!"

"Mary, my dear," Dr. Jamieson said gruffly, "if there was,

believe me, I would already have done it. No similar cases have come to light in the vicinity. The complaint remains a complete mystery. It is most frustrating." He sighed heavily and then leaned forward and took my hands in his. "Mary, your father is an old man whose heart has been weak for years. . . ."

I snatched my hands away and stood up, discomfited beyond endurance. "You think he's going to die!" I exclaimed, a sob breaking in my voice.

Dr. Jamieson slowly shook his head. "I merely meant to say that you must try to prepare yourself for the possibility, my dear. It is by no means certain that your father has lost his battle with this affliction. But no one can fight the battle for him."

I took my seat once more, ashamed of my frantic outburst. "Of course," I agreed. "I understand. But we must try to remain positive. After all, Father is finding strength from somewhere to hold on."

Dr. Jamieson smiled. "That's true enough," he said. "And between you and Mrs. Frobisher, he is getting the best of care. We can do no more."

10TH NOVEMBER 1918

It is not yet dawn, but I shall get no more sleep. I awoke just now with tears upon my cheeks.

140

In the dream I just had, Father and I stood together on
deck of an ancient ship. The enormous sky above us was
heavy and bruised by rolling thunder; rain began hammering
down on us like stones. The waves swelled higher until the
deck swayed beneath us. Yet still we stood, hand in hand,
facing the tempest together. Ahead I saw a wave so great my
heart seemed to shrink within my chest. And as it hit us, I
felt Father's hand slip from mine, though I gripped his fingers with all my might. I watched him slowly fall away from
me—and as he sank into the dark depths of the ocean, his
dear face seemed to transform. I felt a tearing grief claw my
heart as I saw not Father, but the once-dear face of my
fiancé, John Shaw.

I had lost my father to the same dark place as my love.

I pray that such an abominable eventuality remains no
more than a tormented figment of my anxiety-filled imagination. For I don't think I could survive losing my dear, brave,
honorable father to such a fate.

11TH NOVEMBER 1918

Once again, Dr. Jamieson has reported no sign of recovery. It
gets no easier; each time he tells me this, the pain of it strikes
me anew.

After showing the doctor out, I returned to Father's room

to kiss him goodbye before leaving for work. "I shall bring my supper up here when I return," I told him. "That way we'll have more time to talk before you need to sleep."

"I would like that, my dear," Father murmured, giving me a weak smile.

I went back downstairs to find Mrs. Frobisher in the kitchen, preparing Father's beef tea. She would feed it to him after I had left, as usual.

An envelope waited for me in the hallway. It was a hurried note from Bathory, apologizing that business had kept him from writing all that he wanted to—but that he was thinking of me—and of Father. I slipped the note into my skirt pocket. It provided me with some small comfort.

There was a curious air of expectancy on the ward when I arrived. Patients who were well enough murmured excitedly to each other, frequently glancing up at the large wall clock. I wondered what intrigued them so. "Has something happened?" I asked one of the night nurses going off duty.

"I should say so!" she said with a tired smile. "Word reached us last night that it's really going to happen: the guns will stop firing at eleven o'clock this morning. It's the end of the war!"

"Peace?" I gasped in delight, feeling the first flicker of happiness I had felt since the onset of Father's illness.

Sister marched toward us, interrupting our conversation.

"The artillery is still hard at work while you stand there gossiping, Seward," she scolded. "There'll be plenty of casualties to come yet. An ambulance is bringing in more this morning. It'll be here in fifteen minutes. I want beds ready and trays prepared." She turned to the night nurse. "Time for you to go and get some sleep, Dawkins," she ordered. "Night Sister won't want you yawning all over her patients tonight."

I nodded to the departing Dawkins and hurried over to help Helen, who was already sorting the trays.

A few minutes later, all thoughts of peace were driven from my mind by the sight of bloody, burnt flesh. The wounds borne by our brave soldiers never cease to shock me. As the stretchers were brought in, Helen and I set to work, helping to settle the men and change their sometimes filthy dressings.

One young soldier—a Lieutenant Moreau—let out a scream of agony as I peeled back the field dressing from a muddied, open wound on his belly. He jerked and struggled with the pain, his trembling flesh where it had been shredded by shrapnel clinging in strips to the lint. My hands began to shake.

Helen took the dressing from me. "I'll do this," she told me, and began to clean the wound. "You try and soothe him. Keep him still if you can."

I stroked the lieutenant's brow, my heart aching at the sight of his silent tears, washing pale tracks through the mud on his cheeks.

Suddenly a loud cheer erupted at the other end of the ward.

"They've done it!" Sergeant Hopkins's voice rang above the rest. "The Germans have laid down their weapons. We have peace!"

"Is it true?" croaked the lieutenant, grasping my hand. "I won't have to go back?"

"It's true," I promised him, hoping it really was. After so many years and so much death and suffering, had it really come to an end?

Sergeant Hopkins was waltzing unsteadily with another soldier, his crutch still under one arm. The other patients— those who could—cheered him on. Some began to sing "It's a Long, Long Way to Tipperary."

Sister looked on, and for once, her stern frown was replaced by a smile that utterly transformed her face.

I longed to rush home and tell Father. This news would surely rally him. But there was work to be done. The lieutenant was groaning with agony once more. His war was nowhere near over.

LATER

I ran nearly all the way home, wondering if Mrs. Frobisher had told Father the news.

She was bringing down the tea tray from his room as I burst in through the front door. "So you have heard?" She smiled.

"Peace?" I panted.

She nodded, rattling her tray so that the teacup sang in its saucer.

"Have you told him?" I asked her.

"And deprive you of the pleasure?" Mrs. Frobisher raised her eyebrows.

"Oh, thank you!" I cried, giving her a hug. Then I dragged the bonnet from my hair and raced up the stairs, unbuttoning my coat as I went.

Outside Father's door, I stopped and gathered myself, fearful of alarming him with my excitement. Drawing in a deep breath, I stepped into his room.

He lay pale but awake, propped up on his pillows. At my entrance, he drew his gaze from the window and looked at me. "Mary," he breathed, a wan smile flickering over his pale face.

"Father, I have the most wonderful news." I hurried to his bedside and grasped his wrinkled hand in mine. "The war is over. The Germans have surrendered; they laid down their arms this morning."

Father slowly closed his eyes, and for a moment I feared he had slipped away from me. But he opened them again and sighed. "Thank God."

We sat together for much of the evening, until I was sure he was asleep. And then I came to my room.

How my heart sings for all those soldiers at the front who tonight, for the first time since they left their homes, may sleep safely, undisturbed by a fear of no tomorrow.

12TH NOVEMBER 1918

The noise that awoke me in the early hours was not alarming. A muffled clump; that is all. And yet I sensed something was terribly wrong.

I struggled from the tangle of bedclothes and hurried out onto the landing, my breath fast and shallow as I hastened into Father's room.

His bed was empty.

With a sickening horror, I guessed what had caused the noise that had awoken me and ran to the head of the stairs. The stairwell was lit only by the moonlight that streamed in from the window above it, but it was enough to see the shape at the bottom. A body, crumpled into an unfamiliar shape.

Father!

I grasped the banister, not trusting my legs to support me, and half ran, half fell down the stairs, holding myself up while my breaths became hysterical sobs.

"Father!" I screamed, but the body at the bottom of the stairs did not move.

I knelt beside him and lifted his head, which felt unnaturally limp in my hands. His face was frozen, and his eyes stared back at me—for the first time devoid of the warmth and love I'd always seen reflected there. They were empty and dead.

"No! Why were you out of bed?" I demanded. "Why did you not call me?"

I pressed him to me and thought of the lieutenant with his belly ripped open. I wished for his pain. Physical torment would be easier to bear than the grief that tore at me as I held Father's dead body next to mine.

I do not know how long I wept. I could not bear to leave my dear father alone in the dark house while I fetched help.

Finally, dawn stirred me. Had I slept where I sat, hugging Father's corpse? Perhaps the sound of the milk boy awoke me, for it is he I sent running for Dr. Jamieson. The doctor is with Father now. We laid him out on his bed, and the doctor is making a final examination for the coroner's report.

Father has been taken from me.

I am utterly alone.

CHAPTER 13

THE TIMES

13TH NOVEMBER 1918

DEATHS

DR. JOHN SEWARD

Died 12th November, age 69. Cherished father of
Mary. Now reunited with beloved wife, Elizabeth.
Funeral, 18th November, 3:15 P.M., St. Michael
the Archangel Church, Purfleet, Essex.

*Journal of
Mary Seward*

13TH NOVEMBER 1918

This evening I retired to my room, hating the emptiness of
the house and longing for the warmth and comfort of bed. I
lit the lamps and crossed over to close the curtains.

Something caught my eye in the darkness beyond the garden fence. There in the gloom, I saw a small glow. As I focused more upon it, I realized it was not a single light but two— like a pair of hot coals flaring in the darkness.

My heart lurched as my mind made sense of what I saw. I grasped the sill to steady my legs. Two red eyes were staring up at me. Demon eyes, the like of which I had seen before.

At Castle Dracula.

Stifling a scream, I shut the curtain, struggling to contain my blind terror. Had I really seen a vampire lurking there just beyond my gate? Coming here for me?

I had to know.

I flicked back the curtain and stared out into the darkness.

The quiet lane was empty.

I sank onto the bed, fighting the gulping breaths that heaved in my chest. Of course I had imagined it. The hours since Father's death have been long and traumatic. My overactive mind has been pressed to its very limit.

How I wish I were not alone in this house.

18TH NOVEMBER 1918

It will soon be time to make our way to the church.

I welcomed the comfort of daylight this morning—even

though it heralded the day I have dreaded for so long: that of Father's funeral.

I drew back my curtains to see dark clouds obscuring the sky but was as numb to the dismal weather as to all other distractions. At least, I thought absently, I will not have to suffer the impertinence of sunshine.

Mrs. Frobisher has helped prepare for the reception, which will be held here after the service. I could not have managed it alone. When she arrived this morning, she bustled straight into the kitchen, poached an egg, and set it on the table, insisting I sit down to eat it before I did anything else.

I obliged, though I tasted nothing as I ate.

The first of the funeral flowers arrived—a cross-shaped arrangement of white carnations from Becky, which she could no doubt ill afford. Accompanying it was a regretful note saying she would be unable to attend the funeral. She has been afflicted by a nasty virus—I pray it is not the same one that did for Father. Helen, too, sent her apologies— unable to leave her shift at the sanatorium to attend.

When an exquisite wreath of lilies was delivered from Bathory, I cried. How I wish he and Father had met. They would have enjoyed each other's company, I'm sure, their keen intellects a fine match.

Dear Father, how will I bear to say farewell to you this afternoon?

I hear the Edwardses' new motor carriage arriving. They are going to take Mrs. Frobisher and me to the church, following the hearse. Andrew took possession of the vehicle only yesterday. They had been so excited while anticipating its arrival over these last few weeks. How sad that its first journey will be such a somber one.

LATER

This has truly been the darkest of days.

The gray clouds thickened as we emerged from the church service to follow Father's coffin out into the churchyard. A grave had been prepared for him next to Mother's. Jane and Andrew stood on either side of me, and I was thankful for their nearness as Father's coffin was solemnly lowered into the ground.

I was utterly unready to face life alone. To care entirely and only for myself. How could I remain without Father to guide me?

But the moment the thought occurred, Father's own voice rang in my head, scolding me. *There are girls your age married now, Mary. Running their own households and starting their own broods. You are strong. Stronger than the lot of them.*

You can go on alone. You must.

The vicar's words seemed to wash over me as I stared down into Father's dark resting place. To see him cast into the shadows tore at my heart. *His soul is in the light.* I repeated this over and over to myself, but still the tears welled in my eyes and flowed down my cheeks. He would not be waiting at home on my return. He would remain here now, beside Mother.

From the corner of my eye, I saw a new mourner let herself in through the lych-gate and hurry past the gravestones toward us. With a jolt of surprise, I recognized Stella. She gave me a sympathetic smile before lowering her eyes and solemnly bowing her head.

"Earth to earth, ashes to ashes, dust to dust; in sure and certain hope of the resurrection into eternal life . . ."

I forced myself to join the other mourners in taking a handful of the freshly dug earth to drop down onto Father's coffin.

As I stepped back, a discomfiting awareness began to prickle along the back of my neck—that sensation of being watched. It spread across my shoulders and rippled down my spine. I felt Jane's hand slip into mine and give it a comforting squeeze. Squeezing hers in return, I glanced quickly around the graveyard, beyond the faces of the other mourners, my gaze flicking among the trees and shrubs.

But I could see no one there. I felt a flare of anger within me. My morbid obsessions were simply too much. How

could I let them distract me from this final farewell to
Father?

The ceremony drew to a close. I thanked Reverend
Halifax and then told Jane, Andrew, and Mrs. Frobisher that
I would see them back at the house.

"Won't you come back with us in the motorcar, Mary?"
Jane pleaded.

I shook my head. "I would like to say a final farewell to
Father alone," I told her. "I'll be fine walking home, Jane.
Honestly. Will you help Mrs. Frobisher take care of the
guests until I arrive?"

"Of course, Mary," Jane answered. She kissed my cheek
gently. "Don't be too long; the rain promises to worsen before
it clears." She turned and followed the other mourners as
they slowly made their way over the wet grass toward the
lych-gate.

Left alone, I sank, unheeding of the weather, onto the
grass at the side of Father's grave and drew my fingers
through the pile of earth next to it, feeling the wet soil catch
under my nails. "Goodbye, Papa . . ." I whispered brokenly,
my childhood name for him emerging from somewhere deep
inside me. "Oh, God," I sobbed. "Whatever shall I do without
you?" I bent my head and let my shoulders sag as tiredness
and sorrow weighed me down.

I sat on, unwilling to leave Father as the rain pelted down
on us both. It soaked through my coat and dripped off the

brim of my hat, but I didn't care. Only when the church spire disappeared into gloomy shadow did I realize that the sun had almost disappeared below the horizon. A return of the prickling sensation I had felt during the service began to creep up my spine . . . over my shoulders . . . around my neck, constricting my throat. I spun around, half expecting—and desperately hoping—to find nobody there as before. . . .

But there was someone standing by the lych-gate. Quincey Harker.

Terror flooding through me, I scrambled to my feet. My legs felt weak, and I had to grasp Mother's tombstone to steady myself. Yet thankfully, I retained wit enough to remember the vial that hung around my neck. With trembling fingers, I grasped it and held it up.

"Stay away!" I rasped, my voice strangled by fright. "This contains holy water." Letting go of the stone, I fumbled with the stopper, uncorking it in readiness for a fight.

But Harker did not move. He just continued to stare, the intensity in his eyes burning into me. I clasped my collar around my throat and began to slowly move toward the gate, not taking my gaze from him for an instant, expecting every moment for him to lunge at me. But he remained motionless, following me only with his heated gaze as I passed him and let myself out of the churchyard.

Still watching him, I backed down the shadowy lane, and then I turned and ran, pressing my thumb hard against the opening of the vial lest I should lose a drop of precious liquid.

The ground swam beneath my feet as I raced ahead, fearing at any moment the grip of Quincey Harker's hand upon my shoulder. My hair streamed across my face, half blinding me, but I ran on. And all the while my mind whirled in all-consuming panic. The dark abyss of terror I had fought so hard to suppress for almost two years had opened again like the gates of hell and now yawned beneath me. Nothing stood between me and the bloodsucking undead that still lurked there. There really was no sanctuary from this malevolence after all.

I tore through the front gate of the house and up the path and then hammered on the door.

It opened instantly, and I fell into Jane's arms.

"Mary!" Jane cried, sounding horrified.

Indeed, my appearance must have been startling. I was soaked through, my coat muddied from the grave. I looked past her and saw the hall filling with concerned faces.

"Let's get you upstairs," Jane ordered.

I felt weak with relief as she helped me to my room. I let her peel away my sodden clothes, replacing them with my nightgown. Then she wrapped the eiderdown from my bed around my shoulders and sat me in the chair next to the small bedroom hearth. Beyond the drawn curtains, the rain battered against the windowpanes.

"Oh, Mary, I should not have left you." Jane sighed. "The grief has been too much for you."

I had no words with which to reply. My mind swam in a delirium of shock.

A faint knock sounded at my door, and I started at the noise.

"Who is it?" Jane called.

"Lord Bathory," came the answer, like a match struck in a storm.

Jane looked at me. "Shall I ask him in?" she said quietly.

I nodded.

She left my side and opened the door. "Come in," I heard her say softly. "Will you watch her while I make her some sweet tea?'"

"Of course," Bathory answered.

He came and sat down beside me, his gray eyes full of compassion. I felt his soft fingers encircle mine. "Oh, Mary, I am so sorry for your loss," he murmured. "I got here just as soon as I could. I wish I could have arrived sooner."

"There is nothing you could have done," I whispered.

And it was true. I knew now that the darkness was truly upon me, that all I had feared was becoming real.

Now that I knew Quincey Harker had returned to Purfleet, it was nigh on impossible to dismiss the lethargy and pallor Father had suffered before his demise as coincidence. And the thought that he had, after all, been taken by the thing we feared most was unbearable. I thanked God for the broken neck recorded on his death certificate; had his heart stopped beating from being drained of the last of its blood, Father would have risen again, a vampire himself.

And yet . . . Father had suffered no bite marks.

How could it be?

Confusion sent my mind whirling again, and I found myself gripping Bathory's fingers desperately.

He stroked my cheek with such tenderness. "If only I could take your pain away, Mary . . ." he murmured.

I felt tears begin to roll down my cheeks again. I longed to confide in him. But how could I? He would think me mad.

At that moment, Jane returned with the tea. She took one look at my pale, tear-streaked face and sighed. "Oh, Bathory," she said quietly, putting down the cup and saucer on the hearth. "What a sad state of affairs all of this has been. I hate to think of Mary all alone now in this rattling old house." She put an arm around my shoulders and hugged me to her. "I will visit you as often as I can, Mary. And you must come to us too."

"Jane is right," Bathory agreed softly. "You should not allow yourself to sit alone and brood. Will you agree to dine with me tomorrow night?"

I stared up into his earnest gray eyes. I could not imagine how I would venture out into the night now that I knew what waited for me there. "I—I should be poor company for you," I stammered.

"I would be happy for us merely to eat in silence, if that is what you wish," Bathory replied. "Just to know you were not eating alone in this house, where there is only sorrow for you, would set my mind at peace. Please say yes, Mary," he implored. "I'll send my carriage for you at seven."

I had no strength to argue and only nodded.

He kissed my hand and then stood up and walked over to the door.

As Bathory let himself out, Jane handed me the tea. "Most of the guests have gone," she informed me. "But Becky has arrived and has asked to see you."

I nodded, relieved that she had overcome her own her illness enough to visit. "It will be a comfort to see her," I murmured. "She knew Father in his final days."

"I'll fetch her in, then," Jane said. She went over and called her from the doorway.

Becky entered. "I won't come close, Mary," she said, sitting on the edge of the bed away from me. Her nose was reddened from her cold and her voice still hoarse. "This virus is the last thing you need—but I'm over the worst of it now and felt I must come and pay my respects." Behind her spectacles, I could see that Becky's eyes were filled with tears. "I knew your father only briefly," she went on, "but I became fonder of him than you'd think possible in that short time."

She took out a handkerchief and blew her nose. "And Helen asked me to tell you she's thinking of you too. Did you see Stella at the service? She said to let her know if there is anything she can do for you."

"Thank you, Becky," I murmured gratefully. "I am fortunate to have such friends. And I'm so glad Father had the chance to meet you."

Jane cleared her throat, looking a little rueful. "Mary, I hate to leave you in such a state," she ventured hesitantly. "But I need to get back to Grace. I'm sure Mrs. Frobisher will see to the last of the guests before she leaves."

"Of course you must go." I forced a smile. Anxiety was mounting in my chest. One by one, my guests were leaving. I did not wish to be alone.

"You will be all right?" Jane tilted her head and gazed at me, a concerned frown creasing her brow.

"I'll stay with Mary," Becky reassured her. She turned to me. "Would you like me to sleep here tonight?" she asked. "I have no shift, and you look so unwell."

I felt a rush of relief. "Yes, please," I whispered.

"Oh, how kind," Jane replied gratefully. "I hate to think of Mary all alone in such a state. I shall rest peacefully knowing you are here." She kissed me good night and let herself out of the room.

"You have eaten nothing since breakfast, have you?" Becky said gently.

I shook my head.

"I thought as much!" She got to her feet. "I will help Mrs. Frobisher tidy up and then prepare a tray." She looked at me like an anxious mother wondering about the health of her sickly child. "Do you feel strong enough to come down and eat in the parlor?" she asked.

Though I was not at all hungry, I didn't have the heart to refuse Becky's kindness. I smiled weakly. "Yes, I think so," I told her, and she hastened out, leaving the door ajar so that she would hear me if I called.

I have taken refuge in the old companionship of my journal.

While I've been writing, I've heard the front door shut behind the last few guests, and pots and pans have been clattering in the kitchen. Mrs. Frobisher has just called up her good-byes. I shall venture down and see how Becky is getting on.

LATER

Becky came out of the kitchen as I descended the stairs. Her sleeves were rolled up, and there were soapsuds on the apron she wore. She smiled when she saw me.

"Supper's almost ready. Why don't you stoke up the fire while I finish the tray?" she suggested, ushering me through the parlor door.

I knelt before the hearth and rebuilt the fire that Mrs.

Frobisher had laid for the guests. I was grateful for the task, and by the time I had the flames roaring once more in the grate, Becky had returned with a tray of tea and sandwiches.

She placed it on the table beside what had been Father's chair, saying, "I don't care whether you are hungry or not—you must at least eat a sandwich."

Taking the plate she offered me, I curled up on the sofa, the warmth of the fire permeating my nightgown, helping me to relax a little. "Dear Becky, I am so glad you are able to be here with me tonight," I told her.

"So am I," she answered as she poured out two cups of tea from the pot.

I could not help but smile. "I didn't drink the other one," I confessed.

"Ah, well, I won't tell Jane," Becky joked. "But you'd better drink this one—my mother always says there's not much a good cup o' tea won't improve the outlook of."

She leaned forward to pass me the cup. "What a pretty pendant!" she exclaimed, noticing the vial of holy water against the neck of my nightgown. Normally concealed behind high collars, it now hung on its gold chain, clearly visible against my neck.

I touched the small crystal bottle self-consciously. "I too like to keep the boggarts at bay," I told her, trying to keep my tone light—though the memory of having seen Quincey

161

Harker here in Purfleet that very afternoon sent my mind reeling again.

"It's holy water!" Becky gasped in amazement. "I did not take you for a superstitious soul, Mary!"

"It's more a memento of a trip I once took than anything," I lied.

Fearing she might ask more about the vial or the trip for which I claimed it a memento, I hurriedly asked, by way of distraction, "Won't Helen miss you tonight?"

Becky shook her head with a wry smile. "She'll be glad of the peace—and the privacy. Normally we use the room at different times, what with our working different shifts—but when I have a night off, we can find ourselves tripping over each other."

"The company must be comforting, though," I pointed out.

Becky nodded. "It is," she agreed. "I'll miss Helen when she leaves to marry her Johnny. I'm sure it won't be long, now he's back home. And then I'll have to get used to sharing with someone new. . . ." She sighed wistfully. "I would so love to know how it feels to have a room all my own!"

"Have you never had one?" I asked, surprised.

"I've four sisters at home and three brothers."

"Really!" As an only child, I had often longed for sisters and brothers. And then a thought came suddenly into my mind. "You *could* have a room to yourself, Becky . . ." I ventured.

Becky raised her eyebrows in surprise. "What do you mean?" she queried.

"I've got more spare rooms than I could ever need," I explained. "You could move in here. I'd be glad of the company now."

Becky stared at me, her eyes wide behind her heavy spectacles. And then she exclaimed, "Oh, Mary, do you mean it? That would be wonderful!"

I nodded. "That's settled, then," I said. "And of course, you will have a key to your room so that you may have your privacy."

"Oh, my goodness . . ." Becky breathed. "I could never have imagined. . . . Thank you, Mary. I shall fetch my things tomorrow!"

Becky is in what will be her room from now on. I checked that her bed was made up and she had a nightdress and towels and knew where everything was. I can hear the reassuring sound of her moving around, breaking the silence that has governed the house in the nights since Father's death.

I sit at my desk, a shawl wrapped around me against the cold. But before I seek out the warmth of my own covers, I shall kneel beside my bed and give thanks to God for having Becky here. Her presence is a great comfort.

Seeing Quincey Harker today has shown, indisputably, that in escaping from Castle Dracula, I have not escaped its malevolence. It has finally sought me out. At last my old tormentor has stepped from the shadows.

And strangely, though I fled the graveyard in terror this afternoon, I must confess to finding some perverse relief in knowing that my obsessive anxieties are now proven to have just cause. The terrible reality of Harker's return is somehow less crippling than the weight of uncertainty I have endured for almost two years.

I do not think Harker would attempt to strike at me here in this house. I know which weapons will defend me, and I know how to use them. He is well aware of this, I am certain. I long to line the windows and doors with garlic, but though plentiful on the continent, I have never seen it for sale in provincial Purfleet. From what I recall from Father's papers recording the battle with Count Dracula all those years ago, his colleague Van Helsing sent for garlic all the way from Haarlem in the Netherlands—where his friend Vanderpool raised the herb in hothouses.

I shall send word to Haarlem, but for now I must rely on my crucifix and holy water. And I shall take Van Helsing's bag from the closet and unwrap the remaining unused stakes brought back from Transylvania. I stored it away there two years ago, praying that I might never have need of it again.

Even then I knew that my prayers were in vain.

Journal of
Quincey Harker

18TH NOVEMBER 1918

I made my presence known to Mary Seward today.

The scent of her blood, running warm through her veins, was hardly dampened by the rain. My belly twisted in hunger at its fragrance, the desire to possess her almost overwhelming—but I forced myself to hold back. The harder the path, the greater the reward . . .

She stared at me in such terror, trembling like a lamb on the butcher's block—which only served to whet my appetite— but she has lost none of her spark. She challenged me!

Oh . . . to captivate her would bring such pleasure! Under my vampire gaze, she might as well challenge the rain to stop falling. To watch her grow soft and pliant . . . to feel her sinking into my arms and yielding to me . . . I would relish it.

But I let her run and gave no chase.

For now.

CHAPTER 14

*Journal of
Mary Seward*

When I arose this morning, I informed Mrs. Frobisher that I would be returning to work at the sanatorium. I had not been there since Father's death and knew that my absence on the shift would have been making extra work for others.

Becky's door was shut when I passed it. I felt a flash of guilt at keeping her up so late, when she was still recovering from her virus. And so I crept quietly from the house so as not to disturb her slumber.

When I reached the sanatorium, I reported to Sister that I was back. She gave me a rare smile of welcome, along with her condolences for my loss. Thanking her, I took a deep breath and returned to my duties.

"Nice to have you back, Mary!" Sergeant Hopkins called from a chair by the window.

"Good morning, Sergeant," I replied, glad to see his friendly face. "You're still with us, then?"

"They'll be discharging me any day now," he promised.

Pleased to hear of his progress, I walked on down the ward and saw that Helen was tending Lieutenant Moreau, the soldier so badly wounded by shell fire. I hurried over. "Has he not improved while I've been away?" I asked quietly.

Helen turned to me with a look of surprise at my arrival. "He had," she murmured in a hushed whisper. "But this morning I found him like this—pale and listless. He doesn't even have the strength to sit up."

Suspicion chilled my veins. The symptoms had the same ominous familiarity I had come to dread. But how could Harker have entered the ward undetected? There were always nurses on duty. "Perhaps it's a fever. Is there any sign of infection?" I asked, feeling guilty at the hope that sprang in my heart at the idea.

Helen shook her head. "The lieutenant's wounds are healing well," she answered. "No sign of inflammation; only this weakness and lethargy. It must be a virus, brought in by one of the wounded men."

"Has the doctor seen him?" I asked.

"He's coming shortly," Helen replied. She drew away from the lieutenant to attend to her next patient, giving my arm a squeeze as she passed. "Glad to see you, Mary," she said. "We've missed you."

I nodded my thanks and then, as Helen began speaking with the soldier in the neighboring bed, I went up to Lieutenant Moreau. Perspiration pricked my fingers, though they felt icy as I drew back the collar of his nightshirt to search his neck for bite marks.

As with Father, there were none.

And yet, the coincidence of Quincey Harker's reappearance . . .

How could it be ignored?

I looked down at the lieutenant, felt the cool, clammy skin of his brow, noted the faraway look in his half-closed eyes—so like Father's. . . .

Dear God, the idea that Quincey Harker preyed on Father sickens my very soul. And now it seems he's turned to my patients to satisfy his hunger for blood. Does he mean to torture me? To take away from me everything that is dear?

I must stop him. But how can I prove that a vampire is at large in Purfleet?

I dare not alert anyone else to my fears—they would think that my grief had sent me mad!

I should stop writing now—banish such disturbing thoughts from my mind. Bathory's carriage will be arriving for me in half an hour.

Do I really dare to venture out into the night? My heart races at the thought. . . .

Damn Quincey Harker! I shall not let that fiend destroy the life I have fought so hard to rebuild. I owe it to Father's memory. And I shall not break my word to Bathory.

I have my crucifix and holy water—and shall welcome the chance to use them against him should he attack.

LATER

I have returned safely, thank God. Though I cannot say I did not tremble as I stepped out of the front door and into the darkness.

I was grateful to have Becky to wave me off as I climbed into Bathory's brougham. She would be leaving for her shift at the sanatorium later, and I could not help but warn her to be vigilant. "Keep to the main route and stay out of the shadows," I called to her from the cab window. "Keep your holy water about you."

She smiled at my fussing but promised to be watchful if it would set my mind at rest.

This time, Bathory was waiting at the table reserved for us in the hotel dining room. It was positioned within a windowed alcove—though heavily curtained, I was relieved to note. Seeing me, Bathory stood up and greeted me with a reassuring smile. I felt glad that I had come.

Our conversation flowed easily as we chatted about his

estates in the West Country and how glorious the landscape was around there.

"Although my estates provide me with some activity—and more than enough income—I cannot sit idle for the rest of my time," he told me earnestly. "I feel I must contribute to the nation in any way I can—use my privileged position, what influence I have—for the common good." He told me of his plans for a speech he was to make in the House of Lords the following week. I remembered Father's comments of approval for Bathory's previous speeches. Bathory clearly had the potential to be a great humanitarian. I felt a rush of admiration for him.

"I'm sorry," he said suddenly, seeming a little embarrassed. He poured more wine into my glass and then topped up his own. "I must be boring you with such talk. . . . I really must compliment you on your gown. The color on you is certainly most becoming."

His quick tongue had changed the subject before I'd even had time to assure him that I hadn't been bored at all. I looked shyly down at the simple pink gown I had chosen and then smiled back at him. "Thank you," I said.

"You remind me of a midsummer rose," he murmured with a smile.

I lowered my lashes, a little flustered. No one had said anything remotely romantic to me since John—and I had not expected such from Bathory.

"I have made you uncomfortable!" Bathory immediately observed, his clear gray eyes now shadowed with remorse. "Do forgive me."

"Oh no," I assured him. Almost without thinking, I reached out and touched his hand. His fingers felt cool, strong, and smooth beneath mine. "There is nothing to forgive."

With a certain hesitancy, Bathory slowly placed his other hand on mine. "You must see how much you have come to mean to me, Mary," he declared quietly. "I think . . . No, I know," he corrected himself. "I know that I am falling in love with you."

Love! Instinctively I thought of John and the wounds he had inflicted on my heart. It was still too fragile to welcome such emotion from another. "Xavier . . ." I eventually managed to whisper. Using his first name felt appropriate, though strangely intimate. "It is too soon for me. I—I cannot . . ." My words trailed away in my reluctance to hurt him with rejection.

He squeezed my hand and gave a melancholy little smile. "I just wanted to tell you what is in my heart, Mary," he said. "Having your company is enough." He gently withdrew his hands from mine, and I was surprised to find that I regretted the absence of his touch.

I felt the need to explain myself. He deserved that at least, having opened his own heart to me. "My heart was broken . . ." I began clumsily. "By a soldier I nursed at the sanatorium."

"I'm sorry," he sympathized, and though he did not press me, I felt I wanted to explain more.

"His name was John Shaw," I went on. "And the John I fell in love with was a sweet, gentle man. But he had experienced terrible things in the war. And then other . . . difficult circumstances . . . arose." My hands began to tremble, and I quickly hid them in my lap. How was I to explain what had happened to John without touching upon the dark, unnatural world we had uncovered?

Bathory waited patiently for me to go on.

I gathered my thoughts for a moment and began again. "John's sister, Lily, became a good friend of mine. She set off on an unwise elopement. Together John and I followed her, hoping to rescue her from her dangerous enterprise. But our pursuit was in vain. Lily . . ." This was still so hard for me to say out loud. "Lily died. Just before her wedding. And John . . ." I dared not detail John's evil transformation for fear Bathory would question my sanity, so I finished as honestly as I could. "John was so badly affected by events that he turned away from me."

"Was that because he blamed you in some way for what had happened?" Bathory asked, narrowing his gaze.

I shook my head. "The horror of it all made him . . ." My heart twisted in anguish as I remembered the monster he had become. "It made him cruel . . ." I finished. I lowered my gaze, praying he would not press me further.

"You poor darling," Bathory said tenderly. "That you have trusted me with such confidences means more than you can possibly imagine."

Deeply touched, I once more reached out for his hand. "Lord Bathory . . . Xavier . . . I am truly blessed to know such a man as you. I truly hope, one day, to be able to return your sentiment."

He turned his hand beneath mine and softly grasped my fingers. "I know you are not in love with me, Mary," he declared softly. "But will you at least get to know me better?" He looked searchingly into my eyes. "You would be made most, most welcome at my estate. Would you consider visiting? As an honored guest—a dear friend?"

Father's words echoed into my mind—entreating me not to hide away, not to blight my life with fear from what had gone before. And I did so value Bathory's friendship. But how could I go to him when evil hung all about me?

With a deep breath, I looked up at him and smiled. "Thank you for the invitation. I will consider it," I promised.

As Bathory's brougham carried me home, my mind whirled with all that had transpired. His friendship had fast become such a comfort to me.

But as I walked up the garden path a few minutes later, my lighter mood fled as the inky black night seemed to seep into me. I clutched my crucifix and pendant. Was Harker out there, watching me? Looking for a way to inflict further torment?

Fury flared in my chest. It was because of Harker that I could not be with Xavier Bathory. I realized that if I were ever to find the happiness that Father had so wanted for me, I would have to destroy Harker first.

I turned to look out defiantly into the shadows, beginning to recognize in myself something of the old Mary, the person with iron determination in her soul.

The person who would, most certainly, act against evil.

CHAPTER 15

Journal of
Mary Seward

Sleep eluded me for so long that by the time I finally fell into slumber, exhaustion banished all dreams. And yet I awoke surprisingly refreshed.

When I arrived on the ward, the smell of antiseptic was even stronger than usual. I spotted Helen already hard at work, up a ladder, scrubbing the walls. She turned to mouth a "good morning" to me over her shoulder as she continued to scrub.

A feeling of foreboding pricked my flesh as Sister approached me. "Fetch a bucket and brush and start scrubbing another of the walls, Seward," she instructed. "We must get this ward spotless. Two more patients have succumbed to the virus."

"Yes, Sister," I replied immediately. But as I began to

walk away, Sister called me back. I turned to see that an uneasy frown now darkened her face.

"Nurse Seward . . ." she began slowly. "Do the symptoms of this virus seem to match those suffered by your father, by any chance?"

Cold shock washed over me. Did it appear that I had carried a virus to the ward from Father's sickbed? My palms pricked with alarm. "Th-they do seem similar . . ." I admitted reluctantly.

Sister gave a curt nod. "Well, we must do all we can to contain its spread," she went on. "Get scrubbing and make sure you use plenty of disinfectant."

Disinfectant! Garlic would be more effective against this malady! I thought. If only I could voice to her my fear: that what afflicted these men was something much, much worse than a virus!

I stared after Sister as she marched briskly back to her office, guilt tightening like a vise around my heart. Even if there was no virus, I was still to blame. Quincey had come here seeking me.

I began scrubbing the wall facing Helen's, working methodically, scouring everything with such fierceness that my mind emptied of all but my labor.

We finished around the same time and took our buckets and brushes together to the sluice room to fill them again with clean water and disinfectant, ready to begin on the floors. I lifted my bucket into the sink.

"How's Becky settling in?" Helen asked, her voice startling me from my anxious contemplation.

I wondered suddenly if she minded my taking her roommate from her. "I've hardly seen her, but I think she's content," I replied. "I hope you don't mind me stealing her from you."

"Of course not." Helen touched my arm reassuringly and then poured disinfectant into her bucket, watching it turn the water a milky white. "Stella seems to fill the void with her personality alone. We'll get along fine."

Sister carefully checked every crack and crevice after we were done. I think she was pleased with our efforts, though we were both exhausted by the time we left the ward and bid each other farewell at the sanatorium gates.

I could hear Becky moving around in her room when I let myself into the house. I guessed she must have just awoken. I put the kettle on to boil to make a pot of the tea she seemed to drink incessantly.

She came down, bundled in her dressing gown, as I was filling the teapot.

"How was your evening with Lord Bathory?" she asked, sitting down at the kitchen table and sleepily rubbing her eyes.

Eager to confide the confusion of emotions Bathory had stirred in me, I placed the kettle back on the hob and turned from the stove. "He told me that he was falling in love with me!" I blurted.

"What?" Becky gasped. She pushed her spectacles farther up her nose. "Tell me everything!" she demanded, all sleepiness banished.

"He wants me to visit his estate down in the West Country," I went on.

Becky gave a low whistle under her breath. "And will you accept his invitation?" she asked.

"Certainly not yet," I said hastily. "I hardly know him. I cannot just go and stay in his home unchaperoned. It wouldn't be seemly. Maybe later . . ." I stalled. How could I explain to Becky the other reasons that kept me from accepting Bathory's generous offer? She had no inkling of the dangers that surrounded us now that Quincey Harker had returned.

"But you do like him, don't you?" Becky pointed out.

I found myself smiling as I thought of sweet, kind Bathory and his earnest gray gaze. "Yes, I do," I agreed.

"Well, then," Becky said, "there's no reason why you couldn't grow to love him back. And your father would be so much more at peace if he knew you were settled."

I poured her a cup of tea and handed it to her. "No doubt you are right, Becky. But Father encouraged my commitment to the sanatorium too. Though the war may be over, the wounded remain. He would approve of my continuing to work there as heartily as he would approve of my being with someone like Lord Bathory." And I took some comfort in knowing that to be the truth.

How good it is to have Becky to talk to. I find myself at a loss, alone in the house once more, now that she has left for work. The night seems to press at the doors and windows. I have locked them against all but Becky and can do no more now than say my prayers and creep beneath my covers.

21ST NOVEMBER 1918

The sweet, gentle John I fell in love with returned to my dreams in the early hours. And it was as if all harm had been undone, all the horror swept away. I lay in blissful slumber, joyful images flashing before me. . . .

Church bells pealing out a joyful refrain . . . smiling faces everywhere I looked, as I walked slowly up the aisle on Father's arm in a white silk bridal gown . . . holding a sheaf of long-stemmed white lilies and roses of the deepest red . . . Father gazing down proudly at me . . . and John, standing near the altar, waiting for me—looking at me with such love in his eyes. The handsome young soldier I fell in love with . . .

The images rolled on, like a cinema film.

Hearing the priest finally announce, "You may kiss the

bride. . . ." John drawing aside my veil for that first kiss . . . me looking upon his face with such love I thought my heart would overflow with it . . . John's adoring expression hardening . . . a harsh, cruel glint coming into his eyes . . . eyes fired not with passion, but with evil . . . his reddened gaze now burning hungrily into mine . . . him bending his head to kiss me—not on the lips, but on the throat . . . drawing back his lips . . . the light from the leaded windows glinting on his vicious white fangs as they bear down on my exposed throat . . .

In the dream, I tore myself from John's embrace, fleeing back down the aisle. The empty church rang with my sobs of horror. Ahead, the great oak door swung open—and Lily . . . *Lily* lurched into the church, blocking my escape. Lily, wearing her own wedding gown, the gown she'd died in—now torn by the jagged rocks she'd fallen on, and soaked in blood from the gashes that covered her twisted, broken body. She shuffled painfully toward me, yet smiled as she opened her arms to receive me. . . .

My scream awoke me and I lay panting in my bed, my body drenched and shaking.

Will my dreams never cease to find new ways to terrify me? I shall not sleep again. I shall sit with my candle burning until dawn.

It has been a long, hard day.

I arrived on the ward to news that another soldier had fallen victim to the virus in the night. I feel sure the whole ward suspects me now of bringing the virus into the sanatorium. Two patients, chatting quietly, fell silent when I approached them. Sister, watching me closely, curtly reminded me again to wash my hands and whispered to the doctors on their rounds while glancing in my direction.

By the end of the shift, I found myself thoroughly disheartened. I longed for Father's wise counsel, and my heart ached with the knowledge that it was lost to me forever.

I journeyed home along the lane that bordered the churchyard. As I passed, I could see Father's tombstone, newly erected, bright and clean among the other, more-weathered stones. "Father," I breathed, "I don't know what to do. The war is over, and still the hospital is full of casualties. I cannot abandon them, and yet I seem to have become a harbinger of doom to my poor patients."

I came to the lych-gate, and my mouth grew dry as the memory of seeing Quincey Harker there flashed through my mind. I touched the vial of holy water around my neck. It would be prudent to obtain a greater quantity, I decided. And the sooner the better.

I unlatched the gate and let myself into the churchyard,

hoping that Reverend Halifax might spare me some. I was not sure how I would explain my request to him. In Transylvania, the priest had required no explanation; he lived alongside the darkness.

Here it was easier to pretend evil did not exist.

I hurried up the path toward the church entrance. The churchyard seemed deserted, but anxiety gripped me as I noticed the weak winter sun already sinking on the distant horizon. An absurd thought flickered in my mind—that it might, at any moment, fall over the edge of the world and disappear, leaving the world in eternal darkness. I banished the foolish notion at once, chiding myself that I was once more giving full reign to my dark imaginings.

The studded oak door of the church was closed. I rested my hand upon the great loop of twisted iron that formed its handle. Its icy coldness stung my fingers as I pushed the door open and stepped inside.

The sheltered nave was no warmer. My breath billowed before my face. But candles burning near the altar illuminated the surrounding walls and pillars and gave at least some air of comfort. The serenity of the place calmed me a little.

I looked for Reverend Halifax, searching the pews and knocking upon the vestry door, but there was no sign of him.

Suddenly my gaze touched upon the confessional box. I felt drawn toward it. Father's death . . . the mysterious virus on the ward . . . Quincey Harker's return from a dark world

I could not explain to anyone else . . . it was all fast engulfing me. Though I knew there would be no churchman on the other side of the ornate lattice screen to hear me, I would confess the truth of what was happening, along with my fears, to God. Maybe He would somehow provide the guidance that Father no longer could.

I opened the door of the confessional and stepped inside, shutting the door behind me. The confined wooden box, smelling of beeswax polish, felt comforting and safe. I sat upon the smooth, worn seat and bowed my head. "Bless me, Father, for I have sinned," I began.

"No, Miss Seward. It is I who have sinned."

My blood froze as I recognized the voice of the last creature on earth I expected to find in such a place. Stifling a gasp, I leaned up to the screen. Quincey Harker's powerful profile and dark sweep of hair were unmistakable.

Terrified, I pressed myself against the back of the confessional box and clutched my throat, my fingers grappling for the smooth glass vial that hung from its chain there. "I have my holy water," I warned.

"You will not need it," Harker replied.

His tone seemed tinged with resignation, devoid of its previous menace. Instead it sounded immeasurably sad.

"I have not come to harm you."

My mind reeled at this. "Why else would you have come here? What do you want from me?" I whispered.

"Redemption."

I struggled to comprehend what I was hearing. Quincey Harker—the demon of the trenches, the architect of John's downfall, the monster who had drawn Lily to her death— was searching for redemption? It could not be true. Half hysterical with fear, I felt the wild urge to shout with laughter at such a preposterous notion, but caution counseled me to listen in silence as he continued.

"Of course, you do not believe me." Harker turned to face the screen between us. His dark eyes gleamed—not with fire, but with anguish. "Listen to my story," he entreated. "And then perhaps you may better understand me."

I found it impossible to reply but acquiesced by remaining there.

Harker began to speak again. "When I saw dear Lily's torn and broken body down there on the rocks . . . I felt such pain, such guilt . . . such immense loss . . ." he admitted quietly. "A true innocent had claimed my heart—and yet she'd chosen a terrible mortal death over eternal life with me." He gave a deep sigh. "For the first time, I was repulsed by the wickedness that had been nurtured in me. How could I have seduced and defiled such an innocent as Lily? For years I had unquestioningly accepted that making her my wife was my duty—a part of my destiny. But I discovered that I'd come to truly love her. I began to anticipate our marriage with joy. Then, with one wretched act of free will, Lily chose a destiny of her own." Harker paused. "And in so doing, she caused me to question mine."

There was a heavy silence. For a moment, I thought of flight, but Harker's speed and strength were superhuman. He could block my escape easily.

"My thoughts were a maelstrom," he continued. "Could I resist the evil instinct I had embraced so eagerly as a younger man? Could I suppress the hunger—survive without the blood? I decided that I must try. I renounced my vampire bloodline and my part in Father's plan to bring the house of Tepes back to glory." Harker's voice was now thick with emotion. "I left the castle shortly after you, Miss Seward. I walked away from my dark inheritance."

"Where did you go?" I whispered, finally finding my tongue.

"For the first few months, I roamed war-torn Europe, trying to come to terms with what I had done, grappling with the vampire side of my nature," Harker told me. "At times, the hunger for blood seemed to consume me—send me feverish. I would awaken to find I had succumbed . . . and grow despondent.

"I had a yearning to return to England and decided to make my way to the wilds of Dartmoor in the West Country, where my appetites would find scant temptation. And out there, miles from the nearest town or village, I came across Clyst Abbey and the small company of monks who keep their ancient order alive. I found myself hammering on their door, not knowing what I sought there.

"I was taken to Father Michael, their abbot. He sensed the darkness in me at once and asked if I meant the brothers harm. I denied this and told him of my struggles. It seemed like fate. Father Michael offered to take me in, saying he believed that the battle to restore the mortal side of my nature to supremacy was one worth fighting—though such a thing had never, to his knowledge, been tried before."

Harker looked away then. "After a while, I found I could not remain there," he went on wearily. "I fled and hid myself away in the ancient catacombs below the city of Exeter, determined I should cure myself. But trying to stifle my vampire side, to allow the mortal side of my bloodline to flourish—it is like trying to stifle Goliath."

I forced my voice to cold steadiness. "What does any of this have to do with me?"

"I need you, Miss Seward. Lily troubles my dreams, but it is you who fills my waking thoughts. That is why I came to Purfleet."

Harker's words chilled me. "What do you mean?" I whispered. "What help can you hope to get from me?"

"You are the only one left to have challenged the darkness and won," Harker explained. "I once scorned you for your certainty about good and evil. I thought it was shallow and foolish. But now I see that it is what makes you strong. You are the key, Miss Seward. My last hope of salvation."

I could only stare wordlessly at the screen before me. Could it be true? Had Quincey Harker really turned from darkness to light, just as John had turned from light to darkness? Despite myself, I felt my heart open just a little.

And then, aghast, I reminded myself of who this was: the monster who had guided John and Lily so callously to their ruination—and was he also somehow responsible for the "virus" that had taken Father and threatened my patients?

His silhouette moved, and I heard the door of his confessional creak open. Transfixed, I watched him rise and was struck anew by his towering height.

A moment later, my door opened, and there he stood, silhouetted by the glow from the altar candles. His powerful frame had grown leaner. I searched his elegant features. The gauntness I found there confirmed his suffering.

He lifted a hand and reached toward my cheek. I flinched from his touch, and as I did so, I saw something like anguish flood his gaze.

"I see you cannot believe me so easily," he murmured.

"No," I told him, barely able to speak.

"You need not be afraid," he told me softly. "Even if I meant you harm, I could not hurt you in this place." He glanced warily at the altar with its golden cross. "The holy symbols here weaken me. They sap my power." He turned his intense gaze back to meet mine. "I will not give up on you, Mary," he said.

His use of my first name felt strangely, disconcertingly intimate. "I *cannot* give up on you. You are my only hope. Please . . . come here again tomorrow." He closed the door of my confessional, and I was once again cast into shadow.

It seemed hours until I slowly pushed the door of the confessional open again. The church was empty. Harker had gone. My breathing came fast and hard as relief washed over me—along with some other emotion, strangely like regret.

What am I to think? How can I believe such a story from Quincey Harker? But why would he tell it if it were not true? What could he gain by misleading me?

My mind spins. I do not know what to believe. I shall write to this Brother Michael of Clyst Abbey and ask him if what Harker says is true.

Letter from Miss Mary Seward to Abbot Michael of Clyst Abbey

PURFLEET

SURREY

21ST NOVEMBER 1918

Dear Abbot Michael,

I have been told that you once offered help to a man

named Quincey Harker. Though I call him a man, I believe you understand his true nature as I do.

He has now come to me asking for my help, and I find myself unsure of what to do. As a Christian, I must despise all that he is. But I must also have faith in forgiveness and redemption—and if his desire to redeem himself and overcome his evil nature is genuine, then it must surely be my Christian duty to help him too. Can you confirm that what he tells me is true?

Yours sincerely,

Mary Seward

Journal of Mary Seward

22ND NOVEMBER 1918

Another two patients have been struck down. Even Sergeant Hopkins has now been afflicted. Unlike the other victims, he was neither weak nor vulnerable to contagion—he was almost strong enough to go home. The doctors are convinced a virus is to blame—and I am certain they believe I am the carrier. Dr. McLeod has called for a formal inquiry to be made. How shall I bear it if I am held accountable?

I am exhausted and frightened and bewildered. When I see my patients lying pale and unmoving in their beds, I find it impossible to believe that Harker is playing no part in their demise. And yet he claims he has learned to control his hunger. And no matter how carefully I search the throats of the victims, I find not even a scratch to betray a vampire bite.

None of it makes sense!

CHAPTER 16

Journal of
Mary Seward

Harker was already at the church when I let myself in. He waited by the confessional box for me, as tall and imposing as a statue, half hidden in shadow.

My heart faltered at the sight of him, but determination hardened my soul. I had to try to stop his evil from spreading. Seeking strength from the crucifix and holy water at my throat, I walked between the pews toward him.

He acknowledged me with a solemn nod and slipped wordlessly into the confessional. I felt some small relief that he had chosen to sit there once more. The grille that separated us would be some small comfort.

I took my seat in the box beside his and gazed through the screen at his handsome face.

"I knew you would return," he said, looking back at me.

"How could you be so sure?" I challenged.

"You are not one to leave a mystery unsolved," he told me.

"You are no mystery to me!" I answered hotly. "I know everything of you and your kind!"

Through the grille, I saw pain flash in his eyes. "That implies you believe nothing of what I told you yesterday," he said softly. "Have you no faith?"

"Faith in you?" I scoffed, thinking of my poor, dead father and ailing patients. "Tell me, then, Captain Harker: how have you survived without indulging your vampire nature all this time?"

"It has not been easy." Harker leaned his head wearily against the side of the confessional and closed his eyes. "The craving for human blood has not left me for a moment. But I survive on blood from animals—sheep, dogs, rats, whatever I can find. It is enough to keep me alive."

"You have consumed no human blood at all?" I questioned disbelievingly.

There was a pause. "Once," Harker admitted. "Not a week ago. I traveled to London, seeking the distraction that mortal pleasures of the flesh can provide. . . . I met a prostitute, and in the throes of passion, though I had not intended it, I succumbed and drew blood." He paused. "She did not object—indeed, I think she enjoyed it."

A blush reddened my cheeks at the thought, and I was

thankful his eyes were closed. "And that is the only instance?" I insisted.

Harker must have heard the doubt in my voice. His brow furrowed. "You still don't believe me."

Agitated, I laced my fingers in my lap and then unlaced them again. "Recent happenings make me suspicious," I told him candidly. "A supposed virus weakened Father before his death."

Harker's gaze met mine. "I am sorry you have lost your father," he murmured.

The compassion in his tone seemed genuine, but I looked away. How could I trust him? "Now the virus has spread to the sanatorium," I pressed on. "The symptoms are anemia and listlessness. Much like those of a vampire's victim."

He flinched. "You think I have been feeding from them."

"The coincidence of the virus and your arrival strikes me as . . ." I faltered.

"As damning," he finished, casting his gaze downward. "I have been sorely tempted," he admitted. "Animal blood keeps me alive, but only human blood sustains the power I have grown accustomed to—and every cell of my body screams out for it."

He raised his eyes again. "But I have resisted. I swear on Lily's soul."

The mention of Lily filled me with rage. "How dare you!" I spat.

"I dare because I loved her," he said simply.

Could it be true? Surely this fiend could not be capable of human feeling.

"What can I do to convince you?" he persisted.

"I do not know," I confessed.

A muscle in his cheek tightened, and his lip curled into a snarl of frustration. Unease prickled up my spine.

But then he went on. "Miss Seward, when I came of age, my father informed me of my birthright. I discovered I had no power over my destiny—no choice about what I might do with my life, not even about whom I would marry. It had all been mapped out for me by my father. I was simply there to serve the needs of my bloodline." There was barely contained rage burning in Harker's tone. "I was told of my half brother, John, and of Lily . . . How I must one day to bring them to the castle. How I must reveal to John his true birthright. How I must seduce Lily into being my wife."

"You could have refused!" I argued.

"Did you ever defy *your* father?" Harker challenged back.

I turned away, remembering how I had ventured out into society only to please Father; how I had then sought his approval before seeing Bathory. . . . And for a brief moment, I had a glimpse of Harker as a dutiful son, unable to resist his father's wishes. But any softening of my feeling toward him vanished as I reminded myself of his responsibility for Lily's death and John's vampiric transformation. "My father never asked me to do anything unnatural," I countered.

"Nor did mine," Harker answered boldly.

"A lie!" I shot him a sharp glance.

"Everything I did, I did in accordance with my nature," he argued. "Only in rejecting my bloodline do I act unnaturally! And yet I am willing to do it. Willing to struggle against everything I have felt, or known, or been taught."

I had not thought of it before—that Harker might be bound by his nature. For him, choosing virtue meant fighting against the evil that infused his very soul. "But why?" I pursued.

"Because of Lily and John—and what I did to them." Harker's voice was low and filled with sorrow. "When I met Lily, I began to doubt the destiny my father had decided for me."

Giving a long sigh, Harker reached inside his heavy black coat and drew out a wad of folded paper. "My change of heart was gradual, I admit," he went on. "But now that it is done, it is irrevocable." He held up the papers. "An entry taken from my journal of two years ago," he explained. "I carry it with me to remind me of the reason I turned my back on my past. It sits beside my heart—like a talisman, to stop me from returning to the darkness."

We were both silent for a long moment.

"Would you like to see?" Harker eventually asked.

I nodded.

He rose and left his side of the confessional for a moment. "It is outside your door," he said on his return. "Until tomorrow night, then."

As he turned and left the church, I slowly pushed open my door and reached out for the folded papers Harker had placed on the polished floor just beyond.

They were of soft vellum, softer now from being carried so long in Harker's pocket. And as I unfolded them, I saw that they were indeed pages torn from his journal. I recognized at once his handwriting—I had read parts of his journal at Castle Dracula when I had stolen into his room in the desperate hope of staking him in his sleep. He had not been there, but his journals had, and I had flicked quickly through them, reading passages here and there, hoping to gain some advantage over him.

The candlelight in the church was just enough for me to make out his words.

THE ARMY AND NAVY CLUB
36–39 PALL MALL, LONDON
23RD OCTOBER 1916

I came here, as my hunger for Lily grows stronger by the day. To remain at Carfax Hall is to be a starving man trapped in a room with the sweetest, most fragrant of delicacies he must not yet consume. And last night, I almost lost control.

Lily came creeping into the darkness of my room in search of me. She did not see me at first, sitting in the shadows. "Quincey?" she whispered breathlessly.

I remained silent, attempting to shore up my resolve. I had taken such pains to avoid being alone with her.

Seeming bewildered at my apparent absence, Lily moved over to the moonlit window and looked out at the grounds beyond. Bathed in moonlight, her skin took on a pearl-like sheen. Her girlish cologne of sweet violet hovered innocently around her in the still air, a heady contradiction to the salt-sweet tang of her heated blood. The blend filled my lungs, dizzying me with desire. I stepped out of the shadows.

Hearing my footfall, Lily turned, tense with shock—and then she exhaled deeply, her beseeching gaze unraveling my resistance.

I crossed the room and pulled her hard against me. She melted into my arms, arching her back, consumed with a passion that clearly surprised her as much as it did me. "This is maddening," I growled. "I must have you." Feeling the sharp points of descended incisors on my lower lip, I began to trail my kisses along Lily's delicate jaw line and down toward her soft, pulsating throat. She is mine utterly, I reasoned. She was born to be my bride. What difference if I take her now?

"Yes . . ." she gasped as my teeth grazed against her tender flesh. "Yes, my darling. I love you. I love you with all my heart."

I froze, unable to bring myself to pierce her skin. Suddenly clearheaded, I thrust her from me—so swiftly, she fell back against the velvet drapes.

Wanting no opportunity to be swayed, I turned and grabbed up my greatcoat.

"Quincey! What is it?" she cried.

"I must leave tonight," I replied harshly. "I have business in London."

"How long will you be gone?" she asked, looking desolate.

"Only a day or two," I assured her.

"Please, don't leave!" she pleaded. "I shall miss you . . ." she added softly.

"I *cannot* stay here tonight, Lily!" I snapped at her, refusing to look into her pained eyes as I moved to the door.

I fled, running from the house like a thief in the night, transforming myself into a bat and flying to the welcome anonymity of London.

I am still furious with myself. Yet why? Because I am too weak to resist Lily? Or because I could not bring myself to bite her? What stopped me? At the time, I attributed it to Father's wishes that I preserve Lily for Saint Andrew's Eve and our wedding. But the truth is . . . my heart cries out against corrupting her innocent soul.

Journal of Mary Seward

22ND NOVEMBER 1918 (CONTINUED)

As I finished reading, the pages trembled in my hand. I had gazed inside Quincey Harker's heart and seen, among the darkness, a glimmer of precious light.

My thoughts darted this way and that. How could I refute such evidence?

"Wait!" I cried, running toward the door of the church. I looked out into the churchyard. It seemed empty. "Mr. Harker!" I called out.

It was only a moment before he stepped silently from the shadows. He faced me then and pushed a hand through his dark, glossy hair. "I can give you no more proof," he said wearily. "If you do not believe me now, I will go and leave you in peace."

I stared hard at him. "Swear to me you have harmed no one in Purfleet," I demanded.

"I swear," Harker replied softly.

"Then I . . . I will help you," I found myself saying.

"Thank you, Mary," he whispered. "Thank you."

Letter from Abbot Michael of Clyst Abbey to Miss Mary Seward

CLYST ABBEY

DEVON

22ND NOVEMBER 1918

Dear Miss Seward,

You must beware! It is true: Quincey Harker came to me, seeking salvation from the evil that afflicts him. I hoped that prayer would be enough to redeem him. But it was not.

Evil does not afflict him like some common cold—it is a fire, banked down deep within him—a fire I could not extinguish.

Harker killed a brother here.

Be careful, I beg you. However much Harker claims he would turn his back on evil, I fear it is too strong in him to overcome. Do not sacrifice yourself to save this creature, for it is not only your life that is in peril, but your very soul.

God protect you,

Abbot Michael

Journal of Mary Seward

23RD NOVEMBER 1918

I have just received a letter from Clyst. As I read Abbot Michael's words, the heat seemed to drain from me. He told me something Harker had omitted. While at the abbey, Harker had killed one of the monks—a man of God! What greater sin could there be?

I have been a gullible fool!

How could I ever have doubted that Harker was a fiend, capable only of evil?

I should have trusted the words of Van Helsing. In the papers Father gave me recording the battle fought against Count Dracula, Van Helsing writes:

The undead cannot die, but must go on age after age adding new victims and multiplying the evils of the world. . . .

That, Van Helsing stated, was their only aim. Their only purpose.

I shall send word to Harker at Carfax Hall that I want to see him at the church again tomorrow evening.

I must kill him before he takes another life—or die trying.

I thanked God for the rage that pulsed in my veins as I went to the church this evening, for if I had not been fueled by anger, I would not have had the courage to go.

The sky was still light as I hurried through the church-yard. I would not risk Harker arriving first, for surprise was my best weapon.

But it was not my only one.

Van Helsing's bag weighed heavily upon my arm as I walked. I carried it with no less fear in my heart than when I had done so to Castle Dracula two years ago. John, Lily, Father—all were gone from me now. But my sense of pur-pose was stronger and I more determined than ever before. This time I knew what awaited me, and this time, I faced a battle against the darkness alone.

I let myself in through the heavy door of the church, the sun beginning to bleed into the horizon. I hastened through the chancel and knelt before the altar, whispering a hurried prayer. Glancing up at the west window, I saw that twilight was giving way to darkness. How quickly the night rushed in!

I concealed myself in the shadow of a chancel pillar near the confessional boxes and, crouching, took the mallet and one of Van Helsing's stakes from his bag. And then I waited, my breath billowing in clouds before me.

I tried to hold on to my rage, but fear rose in me, growing

like a vine, entwining my legs and arms in its icy tendrils until I wondered if it would bind me till I could not move. "Dear God," I prayed. "Give me the strength to overcome this devil!"

But how could I conquer him where others couldn't? I knew how strong he was. What chance did I have of overpowering him?

Iron clanked. Someone was turning the handle of the front door.

Harker?

I held my breath, frightened that the tiniest sound might alert him. My heart pounded in my chest. Faintness made my head swim. I risked a breath, then another as I recognized the tall figure that slipped through the door and closed it behind him.

"Miss Seward?"

His voice was like a knife piercing my chest, sending fear like pain shooting through my body.

Did he know I was here? Could he scent me? I backed farther into the shadows and listened as his footsteps proceeded cautiously up the aisle. They echoed on the stone, then grew muffled as he reached the carpeted chancel. I could spy him now as he approached the candlelit altar.

My muscles tightened, ready for the attack, urging me to spring and fight, but I held back until he was near enough to reach in a single lunge.

He looked around, his gaze darkened by a frown.

"Miss *Seward*." His voice was more insistent this time. Sharper-edged. He was suspicious.

Another moment and he would scent me for certain.

I could not risk a second longer in the shadows.

With a banshee scream, I leapt from my hiding place and swung the stake like a club, catching him on the back of his head.

Harker sprawled forward onto the steps of the altar and twisted instinctively to see his attacker. His eyes were glazed with surprise, stunned by the well-aimed blow that had floored him.

Swinging the stake up in the air, I caught it and clasped it point down, the mallet ready in my other hand. I leapt astride Harker as he lay dazed upon the altar steps and pressed the point of the stake against his heart. Lifting the mallet, I prepared to strike the death blow.

Harker grasped my wrist with an iron grip. The church might have sapped him of some of his power, but he was strong still.

He stared up at me, his gaze clearing to reveal utter astonishment. "Why?" he gasped

"You lied, you devil," I spat. "You learned nothing at the monastery! You killed one of the monks there! I should never have doubted your true nature."

Dismay froze his face, as though he searched for words he could not find.

"I wrote to Father Michael!" I stormed on. "He told me what you chose not to reveal!"

He groaned, twisting his face from me. "How could I tell you such a shameful thing?"

Was that remorse I glimpsed in his bottomless gaze? No!

I had fallen for his pretense before.

I pressed the point of the stake harder into his chest. "You will not persuade me this time."

Harker removed his hand from my arm.

I stared down at him, startled at his acquiescence. Was he truly prepared to die? As he gazed back at me, his pupils widened, opening into black pools that drew me in

I did not feel the mallet slip from my hand, only heard it clatter onto the stone—a distant noise that held no meaning for me. I felt the rough wood of the stake brush against my palm as it fell from my grasp. And then I felt Harker's strong arms encircling me, lifting me to my feet as he stood up and pressed me close against him.

The smell of him intoxicated me, and the sensation of his body hard against mine made my heart quicken with an anticipation that I cannot, even now, describe. My mind was empty of all thoughts, my body alive with sensation. I lifted my chin to look up into his face, search out that gaze once more that had so electrified me.

I saw my desire reflected there. And all I wanted was for

him to keep holding me, to return the passion that beat inside me like a swan's wing pounding the water, lifting into flight.

He let me go.

The surprise of it brought me to my senses, and I staggered away from him, my head swimming.

"Do you believe now that I am sincere in my wish to change, Miss Seward?" Harker asked quietly.

"D-do I believe you?" I repeated stupidly, my mind desperately trying to take hold of the meaning of what had passed. I searched his eyes for a sign of that hypnotic stare, but it was as though he had shut a door upon me.

"I could have killed you just now, drunk your blood, broken your neck—done anything I desired with you," he murmured. "But I did not. Is that enough to prove to you my sincerity?"

I stared at him, not knowing what to say. Was it enough? Or was he still playing tricks on me? "I—I don't know. . . ."

A great sadness seemed to sweep over him, and he looked away from me. "Then I can do no more, Miss Seward." He sighed. "There is no hope left for me."

He turned sharply, his great black coat billowing as he strode down the aisle and out of the church.

"Dear God!" I breathed.

I gathered up the stake and mallet, which lay on the floor

where I had dropped them, and thrust them back into Van
Helsing's bag.

The house was empty when I returned. Becky had left
already for her shift, but I welcomed the solitude. I needed
time to think.

Harker had not been completely honest with me about
what had happened at the monastery—but did that make
everything he had told me a lie? If he had come here to
destroy me, he could have done so in the church. Yet he had
spared me. Did that prove him honest in his claim to seek
redemption?

Bewilderment crowds me still.

25TH NOVEMBER 1918

I dreamed I was once again at Carfax Hall with Lily, in those
days when we were blissfully unaware of the perils we
faced—she in love with Quincey Harker, me in love with
John—both of us unaware that they were half brothers and
progeny of the house of Tepes. In my waking hours, that
time seems so long ago—but in my dream, I was living it
again. And this time, I knew of Harker's true nature.

I watched as Lily, innocent and fresh as the flower she
was named after, ran up to the house from the gardens,

carrying a dozen or so freshly cut blooms. She flitted past me, unaware of my presence. My skirt fluttered in the breeze of her passing, the heady perfume of the roses she carried lingering in the air.

I turned to follow her—and saw Harker, standing in the shadows of the hallway. He watched Lily climb the stairs, then turned and smiled at me. The intensity of his gaze filled me with foreboding. I wanted to run after Lily, warn her of his dark secret—but my legs would not move and my voice had no strength. I was utterly powerless and could only watch, horrified, as Harker strode up the stairs toward her room.

My desperation must have forced itself upon the dream, for suddenly I, too, was in Lily's room. But now it was night-time. Lily lay slumbering in her bed, her dark hair clouded across her pillow, her lips parted slightly as her breast rose and fell with her gentle, even breathing. What relief I felt to see her safe!

And then, without warning, a shadow fell across her. Harker. Once more I tried to call out—to warn Lily—but I could not. I was like a creature preserved in glass, powerless to do anything but watch as Harker sat down beside her and reached out to ease the dark curtain of hair away from her soft white neck.

Rage pulsed through my veins as he slowly traced the outline of Lily's face and then trailed his fingertips lower, along the base of her throat, a predatory smile upon his lips. I sucked in a deep, painful breath as I watched him lower his head toward her. I steeled myself to witness the bite that would defile her. . . .

But no strong white fangs pierced her flesh; no crimson blood pulsed out of her. I stared in shock as Quincey pressed an innocent kiss to Lily's cheek and then another to her forehead—with such tenderness that my heart ached at the sight of it.

As he drew away to smile down at Lily's sleeping form, I felt dazzled by the love I saw in those fathomless eyes of his. He then turned and left the room.

Oh, what am I to believe? That this dream is a visitation of the truth? How can it be so? I know Quincey Harker to be a monster!

And yet . . .

Doubt had risen in him even while he'd seduced Lily. I'd seen it recorded in the pages from his journal of that time. And it was he who helped me flee the castle. I could not lift the heavy door that barred my escape, but he came and lifted it for me. Without that act of mercy, Grace and I would never have escaped that wicked place.

Twice now he has spared me.

And now he asks for my help.

Dawn is some time away, and weariness drags at my bones. I will sleep now, soothed by the strange release I have found in my dream. But tomorrow I shall visit Carfax Hall and find out once and for all whether he truly wishes to turn away from the darkness. For if what he says is true and I am the only one who can help him, how can I turn my back on him?

LATER

The sanatorium's inquiry into the source of the virus has begun. This afternoon, Dr. McLeod and two of his colleagues interrogated me about Father's illness. They asked when it had first afflicted him, how it had affected him, what precautions I had taken to prevent carrying it onto the ward. I left the interview room drained and miserable.

Helen was waiting for me in the corridor outside. "How did it go?" she asked anxiously.

"I told them all I could," I answered.

"And do they really think you are to blame for the virus?" she asked sympathetically.

"They can think of no other explanation," I replied.

For now, I shall put that worry to the back of my mind and concentrate on the next matter at hand—my visit to Carfax Hall.

The Hall loomed beyond the solid stone walls that surround its grounds. The sun was low in the sky. I knew Harker would be waking by now. As I pushed open the great oak-and-iron gates, I remembered the first time I had called here—to tell Lily that John was wounded and in the sanatorium. I had approached the hall then with no little trepidation, awed by its gloomy facade. I recalled how the heavy rain and glowering clouds had done little to lighten my mood. I felt no less wary now.

Harker has spared me thus far; why would he harm me now? I tried to reassure myself with reasoning—but it felt like approaching a leopard's cage. Could Quincey Harker ever be tamed?

The bellpull was grimy with disuse. I was thankful for my gloves as I rang it. The sound of it echoed in the house beyond the cobweb-shrouded door.

My heart quickened as I heard footsteps approaching down the hallway inside. A moment's hesitation and then the great door swung wide. Harker loomed above me upon the threshold.

He searched my face. "Have you come to try once more to kill me?" he asked finally.

"I have come to talk to you," I answered.

"Are you willing to help me?" he asked.

"I don't know if I can," I told him. "But I had to come. There is something I still need to know."

He beckoned me in and led me to the shuttered parlor. Candles blazed on the mantel, illuminating the room, but there was no fire lit in the hearth.

I looked around me. Every piece of furniture, every ornament sat eerily where last I had seen it, more than two years ago. But now, dust and cobwebs dulled them all and the cold air smelled dank and stale. My body stiff with tension, I sat down on the musty couch and had to suppress a cough as dust from it rose up and caught in my throat.

"May I fetch you a drink?" Harker offered.

"No!" I answered sharply. "This is not a social visit."

Harker smiled, but the expression in his eyes was bleak. He seated himself on a leather armchair opposite me. "No, I suppose it is not," he agreed. "What is it you have come to ask?" He looked weary, his eyes upon me, waiting.

"What makes you think you can fight the evil within you? You killed a monk at the monastery," I accused. "A man of God!"

I saw his shoulders sag. "It is true," he admitted. He rubbed his eyes, pausing for long seconds before speaking again. "It was Saint Andrew's Eve," he said finally. "When the darkness is at its most potent. The evil rose like a tide within me, and perhaps I might have resisted it, but I was provoked. Brother Stephen sought my destruction. He came into my cell with a mallet and stake. Only Father Michael believed I could be saved."

"He does not believe it now," I informed Harker. "He thinks you are beyond mortal help."

"Do you agree with him?" Harker's voice was laced with pain.

"I do not know," I answered honestly. "Finish your story."

Harker stood and turned to face the mantel as he went on. "Brother Stephen came into my cell, intent on my destruction. And though I had been given a sleeping draft that night, some part of me sensed his purpose and I awoke to find him standing over me, holding a stake above my heart. How was I to resist such provocation—and on such a night?"

"You make excuses!" I challenged. "Did you feed from him?" The air between us seemed to grow heavier as I waited for his answer. "Did you feed from him?" I insisted.

Harker lifted his gaze to mine, and I saw it flare with some dark emotion I could not name. My skin prickled with fear.

"Yes," he replied quietly.

Nausea rose in my throat.

"I will keep nothing from you now, Miss Seward," he continued. "The sound of Brother Stephen's pounding blood echoed around me in that tiny cell, the sweet smell of it leaching out from his pores. . . . I was so starved of it. . . ." He paused and ran his fingers agitatedly through his dark hair. In the silence, I felt sure he must be able to hear the thud of my heart. But if he did, he ignored it. "Truly, I do not know whether it was self-preservation or . . . bloodlust . . . that finally drove me to do it," he said, his voice now seeming to crack.

The vulnerability that possessed Harker's face seemed so alien to his proud, aristocratic features. I found myself shockingly moved by it. I remembered our conversations in the church, how I had heard, in his confessions, the voice of a dutiful son and of a grief-stricken lover. Now I heard the self-recrimination of a murderer, and despite myself, I felt sympathy for his pain.

"Tell me," I said to him. "Were you truthful when you said you'd taken no other human life since killing Brother Stephen?"

"Yes." Harker's answer was immediate and firm.

And I believed him.

He was telling the truth. I felt it in my own soul.

I stood up briskly and brushed the dust from my skirt. Sentiment was of no use to us if we were to fight the devil within him. "I will do what I can to help you," I stated. "Tomorrow night, once my lodger has left for her night shift at the sanatorium, I shall return—and shall sit with you till the dawn."

His eyes lit with cautious relief. "Are you not afraid?" he asked quietly.

"I will come well protected, Quincey," I warned him.

He nodded and then gave a weary smile. "You know, I had wondered if I would ever hear you speak my name," he observed. "Thank you, Mary."

CHAPTER 17

I slept long and soundly last night and awoke refreshed. As I worked on the ward today, I waited for doubt to prick me, but it did not.

I waved Becky off to her shift in the evening, expecting fear to rise in my breast at the night's work ahead, but again, it did not.

Determination sits like a rock in my belly, hard and cold and unmoving.

Now that Becky had gone, I prepared for the evening ahead. I took down a volume from Father's bookshelves— Dickens's last novel. We would need some distraction for the long night before us. And then I set off for Carfax Hall.

Quincey opened the door as soon as I rang the bell. He looked paler than usual and tired, but his eyes were filled with relief. "I thought you might have changed your mind," he said quietly.

I brushed past him, wielding the book I had brought. "I

hope you have plenty of candles," I told him. "I don't intend to ruin my eyes trying to make out the words."

"I have candles enough."

Did I hear amusement in his voice? I hoped so; something told me there was a grim task ahead, and any comfort would help.

As I entered the parlor, I gasped in astonishment. How changed it was. A fire was burning in the grate, and every smear of dust had been removed.

"If we are to sit here night after night, then we might as well be comfortable," Quincey commented mildly.

I sat upon the same sofa as before and found that some of the dust had been beaten from it also.

Quincey took candles from the mantel and put them on the table beside me. "To light your book," he explained.

"You will need some too," I informed him. "We shall share the reading."

He smiled. "You would not prefer to play cards?" he offered.

"Tomorrow night, perhaps," I answered.

We took it in turns, each reading a chapter and passing the book to the other. As the night drew on, Quincey struggled more and more to focus on the words, his face growing strained and anxious.

"Shall we stop?" I asked him as he stumbled over a sentence.

"No!" he snapped back. He closed his eyes for a moment.

"I'm sorry. The craving for blood . . . it feels like fire in my veins," he explained, his voice thick with pain. "Let's continue." He went back to reading and I listened, my reluctant heart swelling with admiration at his strength of will.

My determination held until well into the early hours, but then tiredness crept over me and I found my eyes growing heavy. I was relieved to pass the book back to Quincey. He took it from me and began to read, his voice so familiar now after so many hours that I closed my eyes.

I must have dozed for when I awoke, Quincey was gone from his chair. I started, leaning forward anxiously. Had I lost him so soon?

I heard a groan from a shadowed corner of the room. A spasm of alarm gripped me.

"Quincey?" I called.

I hurried over and saw him, crouched there, doubled up and moaning quietly. His temples were wet with perspiration.

"What can I do?" I asked, anxious to help but afraid to bend closer.

I reached out a hand to him, and he flinched like a branded steer. "Stay away!" he hissed. He pressed himself against the wall, his face twisted into a snarl, and I heard a threatening growl rumble in his throat.

I shied backward, reaching instinctively for the crucifix and pendant at my throat, acutely conscious of the danger I was in. What if he could not resist this agonizing hunger?

Who would he turn to but me to satisfy it? "What can I do?" I asked, my voice trembling.

"Take off that crucifix!" he hissed. "The weaker I grow, the more such things torment me."

Quickly I lifted its chain from my neck and laid it on the mantel. I returned to Quincey's side, knowing that my pendant of holy water, still dangling at my throat, would not harm him so long as it was safely stoppered. His growling and trembling subsided. I took his arm gently and drew him up, helping him back to his seat beside the fire.

Stiffly he lowered himself into his chair. I could tell from his labored breathing that he must be fighting unimaginable pain.

"Please tell me what I can do!" I demanded.

"Nothing," he rasped. "The pain must be borne."

"Is there any nourishment I might bring you?" I asked, dreading the answer. I prayed he would not ask for the blood of some poor animal to slake his thirst.

"Nothing."

I could only kneel at his feet and let him grip my hand tightly as he endured his agony.

And then, haltingly, he began to speak. "I have wandered the world these past two years in utter isolation, Mary," he murmured. "At first, I thought the pain of it would kill me. I am not used to loneliness. My privileged position as part of Dracula's bloodline left me wanting for nothing. But only myself and John remain now, and his existence is a reminder of the misery I helped create—of how little is left to me."

A sigh escaped my lips at the mention of John's name.

Quincey looked at me. "I am sorry for my part in taking him away from you." His voice was now barely a whisper.

"I thought I would always blame you," I admitted. The candlelight flickered on the walls. Nothing else stirred but for our breathing. And in the quietness, I was suddenly aware that the rage I had nurtured against Quincey had calmed. "But he accepted Mina's bloody kiss. He participated in his own transformation. And for that, he must be held accountable himself."

We sat in silence, Quincey's grip tightening and loosening as his pain ebbed and flowed. Time seemed to creep past with such slowness, I thought morning would never come. And then, as though a veil were lifted, his suffering seemed to ease. His pain-clouded gaze seemed to clear.

I saw that dawn was nearing.

His grip on my hand loosened, and he spoke to me once more. "Mary?" he breathed.

I laced my fingers with his. "I'm still here," I told him. I took a handkerchief and wiped the moisture from his pale brow.

"Thank you," he murmured.

"I wish I could have done more," I said.

"You stayed," he replied. "That was enough."

He got up wearily from his chair and helped me gently to my feet. Kneeling by his chair had left my legs stiff and numb, and I clung to his arm for a moment while I gained my balance.

"I will go to my bed now, Mary," he told me. "Will you be safe returning home?"

I nodded. Though dawn was not yet lighting the sky outside, I found I had no fear of the dark. "I'll come again tonight," I promised.

He lifted my hand to his lips and kissed it gently. "I was not wrong to trust in you," he breathed.

I returned home in the pre-dawn grayness, being careful to slip quietly into the house. Becky would be not long back from her shift and would be fast asleep by now. For the first time, I was relieved she worked nights. How would I explain my absences if she did not?

I have managed to snatch an hour's sleep before going to work myself. Tonight, when I return to Carfax Hall, I shall go armed with a new weapon—not from Van Helsing's bag, but from Father's old medical bag.

27TH NOVEMBER 1918

I had hoped to steal another short sleep after work today, but the virus has made us busy on the ward and I did not leave until late. Becky was already awake and bustling around the kitchen when I returned. She would have worried about me if I had gone straight to my bed, so I sat with her as she prepared tea.

"A letter arrived for you from Lord Bathory this morning," she said with a grin and a mischievous twinkle in her eye.

"R-really?" I stammered. A pang of guilt shot through me. I had been so consumed by Quincey's problems that I had not given much thought at all to Bathory these past few days.

"At least I think it's from him—it's postmarked from Devon," Becky added. "I've put it on the hall table." She went to fetch the butter from the pantry. "Have you decided whether to accept his offer to visit him there?" she called over her shoulder.

I stood up and began to gather plates and cutlery for the table. "Not yet," I stalled. "There's still so much to do at the sanatorium."

"But still, it is nice to be asked," Becky observed, setting the butter down beside the bread on the kitchen table.

"Yes." I sighed. I leaned across the table and laid a plate before her, silently vowing to read the letter from Bathory as soon as I could.

Becky chattered cheerfully while we ate tea together, and I felt ashamed that I longed for her to go to work, the dear soul. I tried to be good company, but my head was filled with thoughts of Quincey.

She got up from the table at last. "You've been away with the fairies through the whole of supper, Mary!" she said with a wry smile. "Go and read that letter. You're clearly bursting to."

Dear, sweet Becky—if only she knew who really occupied my thoughts.

As soon as she had left for work, I thrust Bathory's letter, unread, into my pocket and hurried to take Father's medical bag from the shelf where it had been stored since his retirement.

I found there what I needed—a small brown vial, its aged label peeling at the corners. I remembered the bottle well, from when Father nursed Mother through her final illness. Morphine. It had given her relief from her pain and in doing so had eased our suffering too. I slipped the vial into my pocket along with a syringe and hurried out of the house. The sun had long since set, and I knew Quincey would be waiting for me.

He opened the door of Carfax Hall to me with such a look of relief. "Mary," he breathed. He looked paler, his face now drawn with pain.

"How are you this evening?" I asked as I followed him to the parlor.

"I have been better," he admitted.

The volume of Dickens I had brought yesterday had been placed ready on the table beside the sofa.

"I hope this will help," I told him as I took the vial of morphine from my pocket and showed it to him.

"Morphine," I explained. "My father used it to alleviate the terrible pain my mother suffered in her last days. He showed me how to administer it and what dosage to use. It might help you through the worst of your symptoms."

Quincey's dark eyes softened. "Thank you," he said.

We read into the early hours once more, until Quincey's voice became halting and I knew his suffering was growing more than he could bear. Only then did I administer the morphine—enough, I hoped, to dull the agony of craving that clawed his body.

I pressed the needle into his arm and injected the drug, seeing it take effect almost at once. Pulling a chair close to where he reclined, I leaned forward and smoothed the dark hair from his brow.

"What relief . . ." he murmured, his voice thick with the drug. "You have made it bearable, Mary. . . ."

As I watched over him, Quincey Harker seemed no fiend at all, only a soul in torment. I felt truly glad that I had been able to ease his suffering.

"When I was a boy, I worshiped my father," he murmured, as though from far away. "But before I walked out of Castle Dracula two years ago, I killed him."

His voice was so soft, so sleepy, that at first the words did not penetrate. But then—

"Killed him?" I echoed, shocked.

He nodded, eyes still closed. "When I told him I was leaving, he attacked me. It was not so much that he did not want to let his firstborn go, I think—it was about my foiling his master plan." His eyes snapped suddenly open and he glared at me. "So, Mary?" he challenged. "Do you applaud me as a demon slayer or condemn me for patricide?"

Something stirred in me—something more than pity, more than understanding. I placed my hand against his cheek. "I have learned something these past days," I told him softly. "The issue of what is right and what is wrong is a more complex one than I ever suspected. Your question is one for God to answer, not I."

His gaze softened, and a wry smile twisted his lips. "I can't believe I ever thought John a fool for loving you," he said. "How is it that you are so young and yet so wise?"

I smiled. "You think that spending the night with a vampire is wise?"

He laughed despite his pain, clutching his chest as he did so. "I think we have established that you can look after yourself," he concluded.

I remembered uncomfortably how easily he had snared me in his spell only three nights ago—how desperately I had desired him. The memory of that passion brought a glow to my cheeks even now. "How easily you seduced me into sparing you in the church," I reminded him.

"I would not seduce you again," he answered, his eyes slipping out of focus for a moment.

To my horror, a pang of regret echoed in my heart. I quickly smothered it.

"At least . . . I would not use my vampire powers to do it . . ." he went on. He grasped my hand. "If I were to seduce you, Mary . . . it would be fairly, sweetly, and out of love. . . ."

Against all common sense, my heart swelled. I gazed into his eyes, wondering if he had hypnotized me again; they were dreamy and glazed. It was the morphine that made him talk this way, I told myself firmly. "How is your pain?" I asked, hoping to distract him.

But there was no need. I watched his eyes slowly close as morphine-induced sleep claimed him.

Carefully releasing my hand from his, I sat back on the sofa. The movement caused a rustling in my pocket. I remembered I'd hastily stored Lord Bathory's letter there and drew it out. I felt a rush of guilt. How disloyal of me to think of opening my heart to Quincey Harker when a man whose character bore no stain, whom I could trust utterly to be gentle and kind, wanted my heart.

I opened the letter.

Letter from Lord Xavier Bathory to Miss Mary Seward

TREGARISS HALL

DOCCOMBE

DEVON

24TH NOVEMBER 1918

Dearest Mary,

I hope this letter finds you well. No doubt you are still working hard at the sanatorium.

Though I miss your delightful company, it is good to be back in the country once more. I do so miss my dogs when I am away. They always welcome me home like a returning king!

The estate business that brought me back here is progressing well, and last night I hosted our annual ball. The family holds one every year for the local gentry. I always dread it, of course—you know how much I hate such social occasions—but the event is part of local tradition now.

Needless to say, it would have been much more pleasant with you by my side, but I braved it alone—and my guests seemed to enjoy themselves. I am glad, though, that the ordeal is over and I can spend more time with my dogs and in my library and hothouses. I do so hope I shall one day get the opportunity to show you the exotic fruits we grow there.

I still wish with all my heart that you would visit me here. But I must not press you and risk driving you away. So in your own time . . .

Your affectionate friend,

Xavier

My heart ached as I folded the letter and put it back in my pocket. The friendship of this honorable man had soothed me, made me feel safe and cherished—yet I had given little thought to Bathory in recent days.

I gazed at Quincey, sprawled on the sofa like a sleeping tiger—wild, untamed, and dangerous. I knew well enough that I must resist becoming enthralled by his arresting good looks and charismatic presence.

It would be dangerous to follow the wild yearnings of my heart. . . .

CHAPTER 18

*Journal of
Mary Seward*

Today went by in something of a blur. I had again arrived home from Carfax Hall before dawn—leaving only an hour to sleep before my shift. The lack of rest was beginning to tell on me, so this evening I decided to sleep a little before going to Quincey.

A tapping on the window awoke me. I sat up slowly, still wrapped in slumberous confusion, and stared uncomprehendingly about the room. The luminous face of the clock told me it was almost midnight. Exhaustion must have caused me to sleep on through the shrill ringing of my alarm clock.

The tapping continued, gentle but persistent—and I could hear a stiff breeze whistling around the chimney tops. Deciding that the tapping must be a branch against my window, I slipped from the warmth of my bed and tiptoed across the chilly floor. I would push the branch aside lest it break the glass.

I pulled back the curtain, and my heart gave a jolt of shock. I was staring into another pair of eyes that glimmered in the moonlight. It was Quincey. Had he climbed up to my bedroom window? Or had he transformed into a bat? Flown here? The thought made me shudder, and at first, I hesitated in opening the window. But the eyes staring into my own were all too mortal, the suffering in them plain to see.

I had not come to him tonight as promised. Guiltily I pulled up the sash—and then, conscious that I had shed my uniform and wore nothing but my petticoats, I hurriedly reached for a shawl and wrapped it tightly around me.

"Come in," I told him.

Quincey hauled himself inside. "Thank you," he panted. And then he hunched over, crossing his arms over his belly as though in great pain.

"I overslept. Forgive me!" I said.

"The hunger . . ." he rasped, beginning to pace the carpet. "How am I to endure it?"

"I will fetch the morphine," I promised, turning to make for the door.

"Do not leave me . . ." Quincey pleaded, grasping my hand. "I may not be here when you return. The night calls me, and I am desperate for blood!"

I felt alarm rise in my chest. "Quincey, you must not suc-
cumb now . . . you have endured it so far," I argued.

I felt helpless as he let my fingers slip from his and carried on pacing, back and forth again and again, like a
wounded animal, unable to settle lest agony should draw it
to the ground and make it easy prey.

"Saint Andrew's Eve . . ." he gasped desperately. "I fear it
will push me beyond endurance! All this abstinence—all this
suffering—it will have been for nothing!"

"That won't happen!" I insisted. "We have found a
weapon with which we can fight your craving. Let me fetch
the morphine."

I searched Quincey's face, expecting agreement—but
instead saw with alarm that a red glow was beginning to
tinge his anguished gaze.

He shook his head violently. "No . . . no . . . you wish to
drug me and let me slide into death!" he accused, his voice
manic and hoarse with pain now.

"No, Quincey, I am only trying to help you!" I pleaded.

He strode toward me and grasped my arms. A cry
escaped my lips as his fingers dug into my flesh. His eyes
burned like hot coals, and I glimpsed his fangs as he
breathed a low, menacing growl. Cold terror flooded through
me. Was Quincey's hunger about to defeat him as it had
done a year ago, in the monastery? Would he kill me as he
had Brother Stephen?

My breath came in quick, desperate gasps. "Quincey," I entreated. "Don't listen to the dark voice within you. I gave you morphine only because I wanted to ease your pain— and still do!" Tears of both fear and compassion welled in my eyes. "I cannot bear to watch you suffer. . . ." It was true.

"Mary . . ." Quincey thrust me away from him and I fell against the bed, unharmed.

I watched as he buried his face in his hands. I had to be strong—for both of us. "You must endure this!" I insisted. "Just as a soldier with gangrene endures the surgeon's knife. Your salvation depends on it!" Slowly, tentatively, I reached out to him. "You must hold on."

He turned to me, remorse filling his eyes, washing away the heat that had threatened to possess him. He grasped my hand in his. "Oh, Mary . . ." he gasped. "Forgive me. You have shown more courage than I had ever hoped. . . ."

My fingers ached in his powerful grip—but I did not pull them away. I did not wish to. The memory of our closeness these past nights bound me to him. With my free hand, I stroked his cheek.

He groaned at my touch and then, suddenly, slumped to the bed.

"Quincey!" I gasped. I sank to his side and took his head into my hands so that I could see his face. He peered up at me through half-closed eyes, and I saw that their deep brown depths were restored to calm.

"It is receding." He sighed, his body now lethargic, loosened from its stiff rictus of pain. Reaching up, he gently took my hands from his face. "Thank you, Mary . . ." he breathed. He brought my hands to his lips and pressed a gentle kiss on each of them. "For your faith . . ."

I nodded, full of emotion. "Shall I come to the hall—sit with you?"

"You are tired," he said softly. "Sleep. The memory of you will be enough to sustain me for now."

He headed toward the window. As he climbed out over the sill, he turned and gazed at me. And then he was gone. I sat there on the edge of my bed for a few seconds and then slowly moved over to the window to fasten it shut. There was no sign of Quincey in the night.

Report of Dr. Jonas McLeod
Purfleet Sanatorium

Sergeant Hopkins was discovered dead this morning. Time of death appears to have been sometime after midnight last night, its cause suspected to be an unidentified virus. A full and thorough autopsy will be required to determine whether this was indeed the case and, if so, to help establish how the disease attacks its victim and by which process it brings about death.

JM

29th November 1918

*Journal of
Mary Seward*

30TH NOVEMBER 1918

The peace of mind that gave me such rest after seeing Quincey win through over his demons last night was destroyed when I entered the ward this morning.

It was unusually quiet. I sensed at once something awful had happened. Helen was stripping the sheets from Sergeant Hopkins's empty bed. I hurried to her side. "Is he . . . dead?" I asked, fearing the worst.

She nodded as she shook the pillow from its case. "The porters have taken him away for autopsy," she murmured. "Sister went with them." She avoided my gaze, and I knew at once that she feared for me.

My thoughts began to race. I felt certain now that Quincey was not to blame for this outbreak. It must be a virus—and considering Father's identical symptoms, I was sure it was I who had carried it into the sanatorium. A crushing despair pressed on my heart; I had caused a death. What would be the penalty?

Helen touched my arm. "Any one of us could bring germs in here—you were just unlucky," she said, trying to comfort me.

"If only I had not returned to the sanatorium so soon," I berated myself.

"And left us here to manage shorthanded?" Helen argued, "You acted with the best interests of your patients at heart."

"Thank you, Helen," I said. "But I should have taken more precautions." I turned away from her and picked up the sweat-soiled sheets from the sergeant's bed. "I'll take these to the laundry."

Time seemed to crawl along until Sister returned to the ward. When she did so, her expression was perturbed. Anxiety prickled in my fingers. Did she know the results of the autopsy?

I had to know my fate and approached her. "Is the autopsy over, Sister?" I asked tentatively.

She turned, still frowning in consternation. "Yes. And it is most strange, Seward," she murmured. "Sergeant Hopkins died from loss of blood. . . ."

Her words struck me like a blow.

No! Not a virus after all.

"I do not understand," Sister went on. "His veins were empty, virtually every drop of blood drained from him."

Quincey.

My mind reeled in horror. The realization came crashing in that Quincey must have left me last night to feed on Sergeant Hopkins. Pain and rage at his betrayal stopped the breath in my throat.

"Nurse Seward!" Sister's voice broke through. "You look pale; are you all right?"

"Yes, Sister . . ." I replied hoarsely. I forced myself to draw in a lungful of air to ask, "Did the pathologist find anything else of note?"

"That is what is so disturbing, Seward," Sister answered. "He found needle marks—in the crooks of Sergeant Hopkins's arms, the crease of his groin, and the backs of his knees. It seems someone . . ." She hesitated and then added, "Drained the blood from him by syringe."

I gripped the foot of the bed beside me for support, hardly able take in this new discovery. But it all made a perverse kind of sense. Quincey knew that I, of all people, would check the necks of his victims for bite marks as soon as I saw their pallor—so he'd found another way to draw the blood he craved. On the nights I'd sat with him at Carfax Hall, he'd sent me away before dawn—and no wonder: he'd wanted time to prey on my patients.

How could I have allowed myself to be so taken in? My

heart twisted painfully in my chest as I recalled the tender gratitude and resolve Quincey had shown me last night.

It had all been pretense.

He had been toying with me.

My thoughts whirled like autumn leaves, searching desperately for some motive to explain Quincey's cruel deceptions. But I found none . . . other than an evil pleasure, perhaps, in causing me pain. . . .

I felt a hand touch my arm. "Nurse Seward . . ." Sister said again, more softly this time. "You really don't look well. The news of Sergeant Hopkins's death appears to have been too much for you. I think that perhaps you have returned to work too soon after the loss of your own father. Go home. We shall manage here."

I nodded slowly. "I think you may be right, Sister," I murmured. "Thank you."

As Sister hurried away to talk to Helen, I fetched my coat and left the ward.

On the walk home, my rage at Quincey grew stronger—and with it, rage at myself. How could I have been so foolish as to trust the word of someone as wicked and calculating as Quincey Harker? I had been so naive—and after all I had witnessed! He had assuaged my fears with a seduction so cunning I did not even realize it was happening.

I had almost come to love him, as Lily had. . . .

Keeping quiet, so as not to disturb the sleeping Becky, I

came straight up to my room to confide in my journal—for there is no one else now, with Father gone.

My body feels weary and numbed with the shock of it all. And yet . . .

I must voice a further conclusion. One my mind had refused to face until now.

What of Father?

If the virus did not exist, then Father could not have suffered from it either. Quincey must have been drinking his blood too. The monster!

Oh, Father! Was your falling down the stairs not an accident after all? Did you use your last ounce of strength to throw yourself down? To save yourself from abominable immortality?

Time wears on, and night is fast approaching. Quincey Harker will come to me; I am sure of it. I must leave here immediately and seek sanctuary in the only place I have left to go—Lord Bathory's house. Quincey will not know where I have gone, and I pray that will keep me safe from any further torment at his hand.

But before I leave Purfleet, there is something else I must do. The autopsy showed that poor Sergeant Hopkins died from loss of blood. Quincey did not spare him from the vampire's curse. Sergeant Hopkins is doomed to rise again and drink the blood of others.

I cannot let that happen.

My decision made, I hurriedly packed a case and scribbled a note for Becky. I could find no words to explain to her why I was fleeing and so simply said that she must spend her time with Helen and Stella while I was away. I would be in touch, and she must not worry about me.

As I slipped out of the house, I realized with a tingling of alarm that I should hurry. The sun was already turning red in the sky.

With my case in one hand and Van Helsing's bag in the other, I made my way to the sanatorium.

Flora at the reception desk raised her eyebrows at my unusually late arrival but nodded me in. I headed toward my ward, but once out of Flora's sight, I slipped down a different corridor and found the staircase that would lead me into the morgue.

I raised my hand to finger the vial of holy water and crucifix around my neck—and realized with a jolt of horror that the crucifix was missing! I had left it on the mantel at Carfax Hall. Quincey Harker had tricked me into removing it!

Every nerve in my body rang with alarm. I was more vulnerable than ever. I would have to hope that my vial would be enough. Praying for God's protection, I descended the stairs.

The winding passage that led to the morgue was empty of

all but gurneys and dusty heating pipes. The gray peeling walls were lit by weak electric lighting that flickered with the fragility of candlelight.

Nurses rarely came down here. It was porters, pushing corpse-laden beds, who most often haunted these hallways. But none were here now.

I pushed open the morgue door. The air felt chilly. Darkness, black as pitch, lay before me. The sickly sweet odor of decaying flesh invaded my nostrils.

Straining my eyes to see through the darkness, I ran my hand over the wall beside the doorway, praying I would find a light switch.

With relief, I felt the outline of one and flipped it on. Overhead, lights flickered slowly into life, illuminating a room that was no less shabby than the hallways outside. About a dozen gurneys were lined up in there. Half of them held corpses. I could see the shape of the bodies beneath the sheets. But which one was Sergeant Hopkins?

Leaving my case near the door, I crossed the room to the first gurney and placed Van Helsing's bag beside it. I could see the outline of a face beneath the sheet, and steeling myself, I leaned forward and drew back the sheet. The unveiled face was mottled with shrapnel cuts and blue bruises, its eyes cloudy with death, gazing blankly up at the ceiling.

I replaced the sheet. It was not Sergeant Hopkins.

I removed the drape from the next figure. The corpse
beneath had only part of its face remaining, its swollen
tongue exposed by a missing left jaw. I gagged at the sight of
it and quickly flicked back the sheet to cover it once more.

Fear was beginning to erode my resolution. I took a deep
breath to steady myself, but the stench of death filled my
nose and my lungs burned with the acrid tang of the morti-
cian's chemicals. I pressed a trembling hand over my mouth
to block the noxious odors. As I did so, a flicker of movement
caught my eye. It had come from the sheet-swathed shape on
the gurney at the end of the row.

I clenched my fists, fighting to gather my senses, praying
that I might have imagined the movement. But no—there it
was again—the twitch of a foot under the sheet. And a little
stronger this time. Sergeant Hopkins was beginning to reawaken.

Dusk must have fallen already. I cursed myself for wast-
ing so much of the day cowering and writing in my room—I
should have come here earlier!

I had to act now.

I picked up Van Helsing's bag and approached the last
gurney, taking out a stake and the mallet as I did so. Placing
the bag at the foot of the bed, I carefully drew back the sheet
to reveal the now-waxen face of poor Sergeant Hopkins. I
remembered how he'd smile and joke to cheer the other men
when despair threatened them, and pity for what had since

befallen him welled in me. I pushed the sentiment away. In a gesture of determination, I flung back the sheet and quickly positioned the stake over his heart.

Sergeant Hopkins's eyes flickered open, as if he were awakening from a long sleep. I gasped as his gaze slowly turned toward me, trying to make sense of his surroundings.

Every fiber of my being cried out against the task I must perform—and perform immediately if I was to stand any chance of surviving. I had done it before, but not while the corpse watched me. And yet I had to. Sergeant Hopkins's soul rested on my resolution.

Hopkins glanced down and saw the stake. He hissed at me like a cat, baring two long, sharp fangs. Swallowing away the rising bile in my throat, I lifted the mallet, and with all the strength I could muster, I struck the first blow. The stake penetrated the cold flesh of Sergeant Hopkins's chest, and I shuddered as I heard his rib cage crack.

Sergeant Hopkins shrieked. He writhed in agony, his eyes fixed upon me, wide with terror. He tried to grasp my wrist as I moved to strike again, but his flailing hand missed its target. I drove the stake deep into his heart. He let out a scream so piercing I thought the small room would shatter like the walls of Jericho. I felt bile and tissue spatter across my face but hammered again and again, refusing to meet his gaze. Sergeant Hopkins's cry slowly gave way to a desperate gurgling, and then, finally, he lay still.

"Nurse Seward!" A shout of horror sounded at the door. I turned wearily to see Dr. McLeod standing in the doorway, Sister staring past him, her face contorted by shock and revulsion.

I staggered back, the mallet slipping from my hand and clattering to the floor.

"What in God's name have you done?" Dr. McLeod bellowed.

Sister pushed past him and strode toward me. I felt the room spinning as shock possessed me, giving me no resistance as Sister grasped me and shook me. "Have you gone mad?" she demanded.

"If only that were true," I whispered.

A smell of burning began to permeate the room, and I turned to look at Sergeant Hopkins's body. His flesh was shriveling into blackness. As I watched, Sister and Dr. McLeod gaping beside me, Sergeant Hopkins's bones then began to crumble—until all that remained on the gurney was the wooden stake and a pile of gray ash.

Sister released me, staring at what was left of Sergeant Hopkins in disbelief.

Dr. McLeod staggered forward, his gaze transfixed. "I—I do not know what is going on here," he stammered. "But surely it is against nature." He slowly turned and stared at me. "What have you unleashed in this hospital?" he murmured. "What is this"—he struggled for words to describe what he had just witnessed—"this abomination!" His eyes burned with angry accusation.

I flinched beneath his glare. How could I explain? How could I deny my role in attracting darkness to this place?

Sister, too, stared at me as though I was the evil one. How could I convince her that my brutality was justified? She knew nothing of the evil that had caused me to take such action.

Had Quincey hoped this would happen? Was that why he had let Sergeant Hopkins rise again—knowing that I would try to kill him and thus find myself expelled from the sanatorium? How he must hate me if he had ensnared me so intricately!

A sense of hopelessness darkened my heart. Every move I made seemed to enmesh me further in the nightmare.

I quickly picked up the mallet and put it back into Van Helsing's bag. Dr. McLeod and Sister did not try to stop me as I walked over to the door and picked up my case. The gore on the mallet and my hands had also turned to ash, and I left gray finger marks as I pushed open the door.

As it swung shut behind me, I clutched my coat around my waist. Then I hurried out of the sanatorium to catch the next train to London.

I caught the night train to the West Country from London Waterloo and am writing here in my small wood-paneled cabin. I telegraphed Lord Bathory from Waterloo to tell him that I was on my way. I will be as honest with him as I dare and pray he will be as understanding now as he has been in the past.

I leave Quincey Harker behind, until I can find a way to destroy him and his black heart.

CHAPTER 19

Journal of
Mary Seward

I have slept a little, lulled by the rhythm of the train. It is now early morning—though it will be a while yet before dawn will arrive. If I put an eye to a chink in my cabin curtain, I can see that stars still stud the huge black sky out there, and a silver crescent moon still bathes the land below. The smooth, rolling downs have now given way to a craggy, more rugged terrain. We must be crossing Dartmoor. I see no building or road. The landscape seems utterly desolate.

Ah—the guard's voice has just called down the corridor outside. "Next station, Doccombe!"

That is the name Lord Bathory gave me. I am almost there.

To my huge relief, a carriage was waiting to carry me from Doccombe's small railway station to Lord Bathory's estate.

"I'm very pleased to see you," I declared to the driver. "I was wondering whether I might need to find my own transport to Tregariss Hall."

"Goodness me, no!" he puffed. "His Lordship would not have guests finding their own way!"

I followed him out of the station to a stately carriage that waited in the yard. The driver opened the carriage door and handed me in. A warm smell of leather and polished wood welcomed me, and I sank into the soft seat at the back. A rug had been placed there, and I drew it around me.

Did I doze again on the journey? I am not sure. But before I knew it, we were passing through the ornate gateway of a great estate. I peered from the carriage window to see the grounds, vast and beautifully sculptured, glowing frostily in the fading moonlight. A great house stood at the end of the winding drive, as elaborate as a French chateau, with turrets and arches and a sweep of worn stone steps leading up to the huge front door. The door was open, the entrance hall within lit so brightly it blazed before us like the altar of a darkened church.

A beacon of hope.

The carriage drew around and halted at the bottom of the

stairway, and a butler, immaculate in a black suit, hurried out with a lamp. Behind him, I recognized the figure of Lord Bathory, coming down the steps to greet me. I quickly gathered the rug from my knees, pushed it to one side, and stumbled down from the cab.

"Mary!" Lord Bathory took my hands in his, an expression of both delight and concern on his face. "It's wonderful to see you," he murmured, "but my dear, you look exhausted."

His gentle tone unleashed all the anguish locked in my heart. I fell into his arms, a sob choking in my throat.

"Mary, what is it?" he asked, now anxious. "Come in, come in. Tell me all about it." He guided me carefully up the staircase and into the house.

I wiped my tears away with my gloved fingers. "I am sorry," I said. "Can we talk privately? I have much to tell you."

When was it I decided to tell him all? On the train? In the carriage? The moment I saw his gentle, kind face? I am not entirely sure. But who else could I turn to? I had to believe he would not think me mad. Lord Bathory, after all, was a man whose mind was open to new ideas and possibilities.

He led me into a parlor where a welcoming fire roared in an immense grate. He ordered hot sweet tea for me and then bade me take a seat on one of the sofas, anxiety still clouding that earnest gray gaze of his. "Now, what is wrong, Mary?" he asked, coming to sit next to me and taking one of my trembling hands in his. "What has brought you rushing to me in such a troubled state?"

I took a deep breath and then began. "I am sorry to worry you, my lord, but I did not know where else to turn."

"I am glad you felt you could turn to me," Bathory replied. He gave an encouraging smile, but his eyes retained their grave look of concern.

"Something terrible has happened," I began. "Something hard to believe—hard for you to believe," I corrected myself. "For me, it is a reality I have lived with for two years, but one that I had hoped to escape. . . ."

There and then I told him all—of Lily and Quincey, of John and me, of the nightmarish happenings at Castle Dracula—and now, of Quincey's return. I even confessed my recent horrific act in the sanatorium morgue.

I did not tell him of my attempt to reform Quincey, though I fear it is shame at the passion I had felt for the fiend that compelled me to keep the secret.

Bathory listened silently throughout, his eyes never wandering from my face for an instant. And though shock and incredulity occasionally misted his gaze, he listened like a man intent on learning. Only when I'd finished did he lean back in his seat and breathe out a long, low sigh. "Oh, Mary . . ." he murmured.

I waited for his judgment, clasping my fingers around his to stop mine from trembling.

"Intellectual curiosity has led me to read widely," Bathory went on, considering. "I have read European histories and folklore that support your story—have come across volumes on the dark arts that describe the creatures you have encountered. But I had, like most, I think, assumed that such writings were based on little more than superstition."

"And now? Do you believe me?" I pleaded.

Bathory nodded slowly. "If you tell me it is true, then I must," he replied softly. "If you say that you have seen it for yourself—a woman levelheaded and intelligent in all other matters—who am I to discount your testimony?"

I let out my breath. "Oh, Xavier . . . It is such a comfort to share this burden of knowledge with someone," I confessed. "Since Father died, I have been alone with my fears."

"Then you need feel alone no longer," Bathory vowed.

I felt a sweet sense of release.

"We must be on our guard," he went on seriously. "This Harker is clearly a determined fellow. I will hire extra guards. And I will be sure that we are well protected at all times."

"Thank you," I replied, the words coming out as little more than a sigh as relief began to seep into my bones.

Still holding my fingers gently in his, Bathory got to his feet. "And now I think that you should get some proper rest," he said. "You seem worn out, Mary. You look like you have not had a decent night's sleep in days. Let me show you to your room."

Giving him a faint smile, I nodded in agreement.

Bathory led me up the ornate central staircase and along a corridor into a breathtakingly beautiful room. "If you need anything, you have only to ring," he said, and gestured to the bellpull that hung beside the mantel. "There is one in every room."

"Thank you," I replied, feeling myself slipping into an ease I had not felt for a long time. I stifled a yawn and then another.

Bathory smiled gently. "You see, I was right," he said. "Sleep now, and I shall be waiting when you awaken." With a small bow, he left me then, closing the door quietly behind him.

I looked around the exquisite room. The huge canopied bed beckoned, but I resisted the urge to crawl immediately under its satin eiderdown and close my eyes. First I pulled back the lilac velvet drapes a little to look outside, revealing tall French windows that opened onto a small stone balcony.

Dawn was breaking, and pale golden sunlight had begun to warm the stunningly beautiful vista beyond, making it seem quite different from the frosted silvery world I'd encountered an hour or so ago.

I let the drapes fall closed again and padded over the

thick, pale green carpet to my luggage, which had been placed by the lavishly mirrored dressing table. I took out my journal and pen. That updated, I shall now take Lord Bathory's advice and rest. I feel I shall sleep well here, protected by him and far from the horrors of Purfleet.

Journal of
Quincey Harker

1ST DECEMBER 1918

Mary did not come to me tonight. Once again, I went to her bedroom window.

But when I tapped upon the glass this time, she did not answer. I saw that no candle burned within. Shock and frustration welled in me—the yearning for blood, squirming and gnawing like rats in my belly, fueling my rage.

I smashed the window, sending shards of wood and glass splintering into the room, and then yanked back the drapes to peer inside.

The wardrobe was open, half empty, and a case no longer rested on top of it.

She had fled!

I went straight to the sanatorium to see what I could find

out. I walked boldly over the checkered floor of the reception area, my footfalls echoing around the walls.

The young woman behind the desk looked up and smiled. "Can I help you, sir?" she asked.

She was an appetizing blonde and not easy to resist. I was so hungry, but I kept to my purpose. "I've come in search of a nurse who works here," I replied, returning her smile.

The blonde glanced at her watch. It was nearly ten. "It's a bit late to come calling, isn't it?" she commented. Then she eyed me coquettishly. "Besides, Sister doesn't approve of the nurses fraternizing with their beaus when they're at work."

My hunger tore at me and left me with little patience. Summoning every ounce of self-control I possessed, I leaned toward her and whispered in her ear. "I am no beau," I promised her. "I simply want to thank her for nursing me when I was brought here wounded a while ago."

I was gratified to find that my sufferings had not entirely robbed me of my charm, for she blushed and said, "Well, then, let's see what we can do. . . ." She picked up a large duty rota from one side of the desk and fluttered her eyelashes foolishly at me. "What is the nurse's name?" she asked.

"Her name is Mary Seward," I replied.

The words seem to restore the girl's senses like a dowsing in cold water. She straightened, her easy manner gone. "I'm afraid you are too late," she said abruptly. And then she lowered her voice. "There was a bit of a to-do. Last night, in fact. She left without notice, under a bit of a cloud."

"What happened?" I queried casually.

The blonde dropped her voice even lower. "No one knows for sure," she replied. "But to tell the truth, I think she's better off where she is. . . ."

I fought hard to conceal the frustration I felt with this young woman's vague insinuations. I wanted to grasp her by the throat and force the facts from her. But I kept my temper and, arching an eyebrow, adopted the same confidential tone she was using. "And where exactly is Miss Seward?" I asked.

She leaned closer to me. "Well, Fred, one of the porters here, has a brother who does some taxi work," she began. "And when he met Fred in the pub last night, Fred told him about the to-do with Mary Seward. And he told Fred that he'd taken Mary Seward to the railway station. She told him she was going to the West Country to stay with a friend. But of course everyone in the sanatorium knows who it is: I have a cousin who works at the Royal Hotel in Purfleet, and she saw Mary Seward dining there with one of their guests on more than one occasion—a Lord Bathory, up from the West Country. Imagine that—a lord! And her, just a country doctor's daughter . . ."

I turned and marched from the building, waiting to hear nothing more.

Fury pulses through my veins—why did she flee to Bathory?

I shall not lose her so easily.

I must find strength for what lies ahead.

Journal of
Mary Seward

1ST *DECEMBER 1918 (CONTINUED)*

I awoke in the early afternoon, feeling quite the most refreshed I had felt in a long time. I washed and dressed, luxuriating in the sense of peace that had enfolded me since I'd confided in Lord Bathory, and then ventured downstairs.

Johnson, the butler, informed me that his lordship was out on official Parliament business. It was an added relief to find that Bathory was content to carry on with his business unhindered by my presence. How discomforting it would have been to have him fussing over me. I was even gladder now that I had come.

"His Lordship told me to assure you that he would be back for dinner, miss," Johnson added as he drew back a chair for me to take a late luncheon in the sunny dining room. "He suggested that if the weather is clement, you take a stroll through the grounds." He glanced outside at the clear blue sky. "The dogs are in their kennels, so they shall not bother you should you wish to go out for a walk."

A turn in the sunshine might help restore some brightness to my soul, I decided. "A walk would be lovely," I told Johnson. "Are the grounds very big?" I inquired.

"They are extensive, miss. But as long as you keep the house in sight, you will not get lost," Johnson assured me. "The keeper lets the dogs loose at dusk to guard the property. But he will not release them until you are safely returned."

I shuddered. "I will not linger out past dusk," I promised him, my skin pricking at the thought.

The walk was delicious, the air fresh and bracing with still a hint of the sea where it blew up off the coast. I find myself refreshed, and as the sun sets behind the trees, I am looking forward to Bathory's return.

CHAPTER 20

WEST COUNTRY BUGLE

2ND DECEMBER 1918

DOCCOMBE FARMWORKER

SAVAGELY MURDERED

Bessie Finch, dairy worker at Nethercote Farm, was found dead in her bed yesterday morning. Her body was discovered by Farmer Henshall's wife, who went to investigate when Miss Finch did not turn up for her morning milking duties.

"She had in the past overslept—she never liked getting up on these dark winter mornings—so I'd gone in to rouse her," Mrs. Henshall told our reporter. "But the sight of her, all white and staring like that . . . It's something I'll never get over!"

The police doctor has reported that the victim's neck was broken—and that her body had been drained of blood.

"I can't imagine who could have done such a terrible thing to poor Bessie," Mrs. Henshall wept.

"I know she was a lazy lump of a girl, but she didn't deserve such a cruel end."

Police are still looking for clues to this wicked crime. So far, no suspects have been named.

Journal of Mary Seward

2ND DECEMBER 1918

Bathory had again left to do his rounds on the estate when I came down to breakfast this morning. Country life starts early, I have discovered.

Johnson had placed the local newspaper beside my breakfast plate.

The headline told of a young woman in the locality who had been murdered—drained of blood.

I did not need to know more.

This was the work of a vampire. Quincey Harker had discovered my whereabouts. Cold dread gripped me. Why did he pursue me so doggedly?

And how could have he tracked me down so quickly?

I walked again about the grounds this morning, fretful despite the sunshine. I have taken Johnson's advice and always keep the house in sight. This afternoon I sought distraction in the library, but Bathory's collection of books proved a little dry for my tastes. Besides, I was impatient for his return, longing to share with him the contents of the newspaper article.

I showed him as soon as he got home. "My tormentor has somehow found out where I am," I said, my voice trembling.

While Bathory quickly scanned the article about the murdered young woman, my gaze strayed to the window. Outside, twilight had bled into evening and the grounds beyond the window were swathed in darkness.

"Please try not to worry, Mary," Bathory said soothingly. He cast the paper down on the sofa, strode to the windows, and closed the curtains. "You are safe here with me."

I pray he is right—for both of us.

3RD DECEMBER 1918

Lily came to me in my dreams again last night. It is as though my renewed anxiety over Quincey has drawn her back to the forefront of my mind—to haunt me with her tragic memory.

I dreamt that I awoke to find her standing over me. It felt strange, seeing her in Bathory's home. Bloody and disfigured, she gazed down at me with pleading eyes and beckoned me from my bed.

I was powerless to refuse her.

As I crossed the room after her, she passed through the door like a ghost. I had to open it to follow.

I saw her waiting for me in the dimly lit hallway. "Lily!" I called. "Where are we going?"

But she paid no heed to my question and drifted on, turning into another hallway, leading me away from the part of the house that was familiar to me.

Some cold foreboding stayed my step. I did not want to follow. "Do come back, Lily!" I pleaded. "I am cold!"

But still she did not listen. She seemed to have some purpose and drifted on.

I followed, fearful of letting her out of my sight, mindful of what had happened when I'd left her alone in Castle Dracula.

I did not recognize the part of the house she led me to at all. A feeling of disorientation gripped me, and my fear began to grow. How would I ever find my way back to my own room again?

At last, Lily stopped beside a door that was slightly ajar. Soft light from within the room beyond it seeped out into the corridor. I opened my mouth to ask Lily why she had led me here—but she silenced me by putting a bloodied finger to her bruised lips.

I heard a whimpering cry drift out from within the room.

My previous nightmares should have taught me caution, but I pushed open the door and looked in.

Reclining on the bed was a young woman, her face contorted in terror, her eyes so wide that their whites shone in the half-light. She struggled against the fiend that pinned her to the bed, lowering its mouth to her throat—and then suddenly she stiffened and gasped as it penetrated her flesh with its fangs. It began to feed, and the young woman's cries became a strangled, desperate choking.

The blood pulsing through my veins seemed to rush to my head. I felt I was drowning in it. I recognized the creature even before it straightened and turned to stare at me, its eyes glittering like rubies, mouth and chin glistening red with blood.

It was John.

His face broke into a gloating smile.

A scream rose from the depths of me and rang shrilly from my lips.

I must have screamed out loud in my sleep and roused myself from the devastating nightmare, for suddenly I was awake.

I was in my bed, staring at its shadowed canopy overhead.

Quick footsteps sounded in the corridor outside, growing louder as they came closer, and then the door was flung wide.

Lord Bathory stood in the open doorway, a pistol in his hand. "What is it, Mary?" he demanded anxiously. "I heard you scream!"

"A nightmare . . ." I quavered. "Such a nightmare, I can hardly bear that my imagination could conjure up such a thing. . . ."

Bathory closed his eyes with relief. "A nightmare," he echoed. He came to my bedside and laid his pistol on the cabinet beside me. Though I knew a pistol would be little use against Quincey, I was relieved to see that Bathory was ready to take the threat seriously.

He tenderly pushed a strand of hair from my face. "What did you dream of to frighten you so?" he asked.

I shuddered as I remembered. "I dreamt that John was here, in your house," I told him. "Though it seems strange that I should dream that John was here when it is Quincey who pursues me," I observed.

"Mary, if any vampire dared enter my house, I'd shoot him down like a dog!" Bathory vowed.

I shook my head. "Only a wooden stake through the heart will kill them," I explained. "And garlic and crucifixes will drive them away." I lifted the vial that hung at my throat. "Or this."

Bathory looked puzzled. "What is it?" he asked.

"Holy water," I told him.

Bathory raised his eyebrows. "Then I shall send a maid to the local church for a gallon of it tomorrow," he said earnestly. "I believe some darkness stalks you, and I will do whatever it takes to defend you."

I loosened my grip on him, reassured.

Bathory remained silent for a long moment. "Mary, this Quincey Harker must be a devil to want to hurt an angel like you," he then murmured. "But do not worry. I shall keep this fiend from our doorstep." And then he bent to gently kiss my brow. It was the most intimate gesture Bathory had yet made. It suffused me with warmth.

"I have to be away again in the morning. More politicking," he explained. "You, however, must sleep in and recover. I shall spend the day looking forward to sharing dinner with you on my return." Picking up his pistol, he rose and headed for the door.

I nodded. "Thank you, Xavier," I said gratefully. He turned and smiled, his expression tender.

Once he was gone, I rose from my bed to fetch my journal. I knew I would not sleep.

Perhaps I will now, having purged the terrible experience on paper.

I slumbered uneasily until an hour or two after daybreak. Bathory had long since left on his business when I finally arose and went downstairs. I had little appetite, but a place at the breakfast table had been laid out for me, and, not wishing to seem ungrateful, I forced myself to eat a slice of toast and marmalade and drink a cup of tea.

There was nothing more in the local newspaper this morning about the murder.

After breakfast, a cold wind rattled the windows; I had no heart to venture outside and returned to my room. I stared out at the gardens, unappreciative of their beauty, my mind questioning again why John had returned to haunt my dreams. My new anxieties had clearly stirred old ones too. I found myself almost as fearful as if I were still in Castle Dracula, surrounded by the demons that inhabited that dark place.

And then a glimmer of sense broke through my obsessive worrying: if I explored the house, perhaps it would put my mind at rest. I reasoned that if I could see all the corridors in the bright, crisp light of day, some of the horrors left by my dreams might be dispelled.

I set off on my task. In daylight, the corridors were bright and well lit by wide windows. Painted in the most delicate colors and adorned by beautiful furniture and paintings, they seemed not frightening in the least.

Feeling relieved to see reality so unlike my nightmare, I returned to my room to discover that a cold luncheon had been brought up and left for me on a tray. Touched by Johnson's thoughtfulness and finding my appetite somewhat restored, I ate the food gratefully.

Now, with last night's nightmare dispelled and a full stomach, I feel rather drowsy. Lord Bathory is right—my anxieties really have taken it out of me. I shall rest for the afternoon and be fresh for his return.

LATER

I did not reawaken until a gentle tapping on my door penetrated my consciousness. I blinked open my eyes with a start—surprised to discover that the sun had already set. Moonlight streamed in through the tall windows.

"Mary?" Bathory's soft voice called through the door.

Rubbing my eyes, I sat up. "Yes? Come in," I called.

The door opened and Bathory entered, an inquiring smile on his kind face. "Have you been able to rest?" he asked, concern still evident in his voice.

"Yes, thank you," I assured him, pushing the rumpled hair from my face. "What time is it?"

"Almost eight o'clock," Bathory replied. He crossed over to the windows to close the drapes.

I gave him a grateful smile.

"I've come to see if you feel up to joining me for dinner," Bathory went on tentatively.

"Of course!" I told him. "I shall be down presently."

Bathory nodded. "Good, I shall tell Cook," he said, and left again, closing the door quietly behind him.

I decided I would change into a more elegant dress—make more of an effort as Bathory's guest. I chose the high-necked blue gown I had worn for our first dinner together. As I struggled with fastening some of its buttons, I heard a noise on the balcony beyond my window.

I froze momentarily, my flesh tingling with sudden fear. Then I rushed to the bellpull at the side of the mantel and tugged it ferociously.

"Mary . . ."

The unwelcome voice beyond the window stopped the breath in my throat.

Quincey Harker was outside my window.

I heard the door handle twisting as he tried to open it. Did he really think I would leave it unlocked?

"Mary, let me in!" he ordered.

What sort of a fool did he think me?

Instinct drove me into action. Though every fiber in my body called to me to run from my room—what would be the point? Quincey would only pursue me. If he had come to claim me, I would face him! But I would not give up my life and soul without a fight.

I undid the chain that held my vial of holy water with trembling fingers, fumbling desperately with the small catch. The French windows rattled louder. Quincey was determined to break in. At last the catch opened, and I held up the vial and drew out the stopper. Not a moment too soon! I heard the wooden frame creaking then cracking under the strain.

With a splintering crash, the lock gave and the curtains billowed open, blown by the inrush of night air.

Quincey stood in the doorway, framed against the night sky, his face glowing in the light from my room. "Why did you run from me?" he rasped, fury gleaming in his gaze.

"Because you are a murderer!" I accused. "You lied to me about abstaining from human blood—*you* killed my father and my patients at the sanatorium! You want to ruin me!"

Quincey slumped against the window frame, shaking his head, as though grown weak.

"There's no need to keep up your pretense anymore!" I spat. "I will never believe you again!"

"No!" he muttered, perspiration pricking his brow.

"Why do you persecute me so?" I demanded. "You have toyed with me from the start! Have you finally decided to kill me?" The vial of holy water trembled in my hand as I held it out toward him. It seemed suddenly so small, capable of no more than inflicting some small wound.

My bedroom door slammed open.

"Mary!" Bathory stood there, his pistol in his hand. Following my terrified gaze, he saw Quincey at the window. Without hesitating, Bathory took aim and fired at him.

At once, Quincey turned and sprang away, slithering over the balcony's edge.

Bathory ran to the stone railing and, leaning over, fired again.

I sank slowly to the floor, relief flooding me. "Did you hit him?" I called.

"I think I winged him," Bathory called back from the balcony.

I had not expected Bathory's weapon to harm Quincey. Pain seared my heart, but I quashed it. I would not let myself feel compassion for that demon again. "Has he gone?"

"He's disappeared into the shadows," Bathory told me. "The dogs will sniff him out if he's still on the grounds."

"But they will do no good. Harker commands wolves!" I pointed out.

"If he has become vulnerable to my bullets, perhaps he'll be vulnerable to my hounds also," Bathory replied. He turned to me, his pistol hanging in his hand, face flushed, shoulders squared—quite changed from the affable scholar I had first known. He gave me a wry little smile. "It seems you have made a man of action out of me," he commented, as though reading my thoughts. He crossed the room and crouched beside me. "Are you harmed, Mary?" he asked

gently.

"Only shaken," I replied.

"If I ever doubted how much danger you were in, I believe it now," he said. His gaze was deadly serious. Quincey's assault had clearly shocked him.

I leaned my forehead wearily against his shoulder. He had saved me, and I found my heart swelling with gratitude. "Oh, Xavier, what would I have done if you'd not come to my aid?"

He stroked my hair. "I will always come to your aid, Mary," he vowed.

The scent of him was warm and comforting, and I longed to stay there, resting against him, but he stood up and drew me to my feet.

I let him lead me down to the dining room, where a cozy fire crackled in the grate. Bathory seated me and rang the bell. Within moments, Johnson came.

"Johnson," Bathory said as soon as the butler appeared, "please have Philips mend the window lock in Miss Seward's bedroom at once. It must be mended securely."

"Very good, my lord," Johnson answered.

"And alert the guards that an intruder was spotted on the grounds. They are to do whatever is necessary to bring the man down should they encounter him."

"Yes, my lord." Johnson left us with a bow.

We ate in silence to begin with, recovering, each of us, from the shock of our encounter with Quincey.

At last, Bathory spoke. "Now that I've seen Harker for myself, I see why you fear him so," he said. "There was such a look in his eye. As though destroying you was an obsession with him. Why does he hold such a grudge against you?"

"I wish I knew." I sighed. "There was no love lost between us from the moment we met," I admitted. "He knew that I did not approve of his courting Lily. Even before we discovered the terrible truth about him, the stories I'd read of his conduct in the trenches warned me that there was a dark side to him."

I paused. "But then . . . for some reason . . . he allowed me to flee Castle Dracula. . . ."

Bathory looked at me in surprise on hearing this.

I shook my head resolutely. "Whatever his reason for that, Quincey has certainly shown me no mercy since. He has gone to great lengths to unravel my life and strip it of all that is precious to me. Maybe he released me simply for the sport of tormenting me now."

Suddenly I felt a compulsion to tell Bathory the parts of the story I had omitted when I had first arrived here. It seemed like a betrayal to keep anything from him now. "Quincey has deceived me at every turn," I confessed. "He told me, when he first found me in Purfleet, that he was trying to fight the evil that tainted his soul. He begged me to help him."

Bathory raised a quizzical eyebrow. "And did you?" he queried.

I bowed my head, ashamed as I remembered how close to my heart I'd allowed Quincey to come. "He tricked me into thinking I could not turn my back on him," I mumbled.

Bathory listened, his eyes wide with disbelief, as I told him of the evenings I had spent at Quincey's side, so certain that he sought salvation that I'd risked my life—even my soul—to help him. "I truly believed I saw a change in him," I confessed. "But it was all lies to deceive me."

In that moment, sitting in Bathory's lavish dining room, I remembered Lily and the desolate look in her eyes when she learned the truth about her beloved.

"I truly believe Quincey takes pleasure in prolonging the suffering of others," I concluded bitterly. "He plays games with his victims as a cat does with a mouse."

"He shall play no more games with you," Bathory pledged fiercely.

I stared into his gray gaze. Dear Bathory! He had forced himself to change—from a timid and bookish creature into a man ready to battle pitiless evil on my behalf. How could I not be touched by him?

"You are my knight in shining armor," I murmured, reaching out to place my hand over his. "The sweetest man I have ever known. I am thankful that we met."

Bathory flushed. "Protecting you is an honor, Mary," he murmured.

I smiled, my heart swelling with affection for him.

Johnson knocked, disturbing the moment. "Sorry to intrude, sir," he apologized. "But I thought you would like to know that Philips has finished his repairs." He raised an eyebrow and added, "Is there anything I should inform the police about, my lord?"

"It might as well wait until morning," Bathory told him. "The scoundrel who broke the window must be long gone or the dogs would be howling."

"Very well, sir." Johnson dipped his head and left.

The butler's intrusion had broken the intimacy between Bathory and me. With a jolt, I realized how much I had opened my heart. "I—I really should go up to bed," I stammered awkwardly, though inwardly I trembled at the thought of being alone in my room again. But I persuaded myself that I would be safe enough there until morning. The window in my room was newly secured and Bathory was on hand should I need him.

Bathory stood as I got up to leave and kissed my hand. "Sleep soundly, my dear," he told me. "The dogs and guards are roaming the grounds, and I shall reload my pistol. I will remain awake through the night, keeping watch for any disturbance."

I pray that these precautions will be enough, though I cannot believe it.

The repairs on the window look sound, but still . . . I have put on every light so that all shadows have been banished.

My journal now written, I shall read in bed—for, like Bathory, I doubt that I shall dare close my eyes before dawn.

CHAPTER 21

Journal of
Mary Seward

The next thing I was aware of was a hand pressing over my mouth, stifling the scream that immediately rose in my throat. I must have dozed off after all. The smothering fingers were Quincey's. Terror screeched within me. I struggled, but his other arm encircled me and pinned my hands to my side. My feet grew tangled in my bedclothes as I kicked wildly to free myself.

"Do not struggle, Mary!" he hissed in my ear, his breath hot on my neck.

I kicked again and fought wildly, but he was too strong and held me captive where I lay. Black, desperate terror unfurled in my mind.

"The servant did a good job mending the window," Quincey whispered. "He seemed surprised to see me at first, but I won him over—enough for him to invite me in," he added with a wry smile.

Quincey had mesmerized the handyman. He had been in my room all along, waiting only for me to go to sleep!

Horrified, I struggled to keep my senses. I realized that I must avoid his gaze. I would not be mesmerized into submission as well. He would have to fight me to the bitter end.

"Mary, why do you struggle?" His icy calm seemed to evaporate, and desperation crept into his tone. "How could you lose faith in me so easily, after all we have shared?"

How could I lose faith in him? I wanted to scream at him, rage vying with horror in my breast. *You lied! You lied!* But no words could escape the cruel grip he had on me.

"I'm sorry if I'm hurting you, but I cannot risk your raising the alarm again until I have had a chance to speak with you. To explain," he told me. "Bathory is dangerous—he will surely harm you if he has not done so already!"

I shook my head angrily. Bathory, dangerous? What nonsense did he expect me to believe now?

"I am not certain how you came to know him, but you must get away from him," Quincey went on. "You must follow me. Now."

Dear God, when would he stop his sadistic game? I flinched in his grip, and he pressed me tighter to him. He sighed, and I felt him press his face into my tangled hair.

"I have lost one love." He whispered the words, so softly. "I cannot bear to lose another."

I squeezed my eyes shut, my heart twisting in confusion as I breathed in the warm smell of him, drawing it deep into my lungs.

His affection—it seemed so real. But how? How could it be?

"Mary, look at me!" he said pleadingly. "See that I am telling you the truth!"

This time, I heard the anguish in his tone. I could feel faint tremors rippling through his body and his labored breath in my hair. I felt his heaving heartbeat as he pressed me to him, and my soul seemed to sigh. How could I help but look?

I opened my eyes and turned my face to his.

Quincey's tormented gaze showed no glimmer of fire, and yet it seemed to burn into me like flame. I found myself absorbed by its depths.

"All I told you was true, Mary," he told me. "I do not understand what drove you from me."

He let me drag his hand from my mouth, his eyes pleading for some answer.

I sobbed quietly. "You killed my father."

Quincey shook his head. "Mary . . . how could I have when I was unable to cross his threshold?"

I looked at him dumbly.

"A vampire cannot enter a place unless invited in!" Quincey explained, exasperation now edging his voice.

Deep within, my heart sighed. I remembered that terrible night when I had overslept and found Quincey at my window. He had not come in until I told him to. Was that the reason?

Tears welled in my eyes as he kissed my forehead, my cheek, my chin. Each place he touched with his lips flushed with warmth.

"I swear to you. I am not the one you need to fear," he whispered, his mouth now at my ear. "Come away with me, Mary. There is little time."

The sensation thrilled me, and a soft moan of pleasure escaped my lips. I felt Quincey's breath upon the nape of my neck.

He bent to kiss my throat, leaving a trail that felt like fire upon my skin and set my body trembling with desire.

Would he bite me now? I wondered. Would all of this finally be over?

Outside, I heard the dogs begin to howl.

Their cries grew louder, closer, as though they crowded outside my window. I trembled in anticipation of his bite, my body flooded with the clawing desperation of passion almost fulfilled.

At once, Quincey wrenched himself from my embrace. "I must go now! Someone approaches, but I'll be back for you, Mary."

"Quincey!" I called in alarm. My heart lurched as he

rushed out onto the balcony and jumped over the edge.

My door flew open **and Bathory** rushed in. He was panting, alarm lighting his face.

"Someone locked the dogs inside their pound and quieted them with fresh meat! I freed them, and they smelled him out at once. Harker is still on the grounds!"

At the sight of Bathory, my wits returned, though passion still lingered in my body.

"He came back!" I cried.

I shook my head to clear it. What had I done? I'd almost given myself to Quincey—again!

"Did he hurt you?" Bathory demanded. His normally gentle face burned with rage.

"No." I shook my head once more. Common sense was crowding back—my mind once more overruling my heart. If Quincey had managed to mesmerize Philips into letting him into my room, I realized that he could have done the same to Father! What an unthinking fool Quincey Harker was making of me. "He is still playing games with me—he tried to persuade me that you were dangerous!" I told Bathory.

"I? Dangerous?" Bathory looked outraged. He stared at the smashed window. "You will sleep in the room next to mine tonight," he decided. He took my hand, and as he did so, reason chased away the last of the fevered desire that had consumed my body when Quincey had held me in his arms. In its place, cold regret washed over me. What had I done—

allowing that demon into my heart again? Offering myself to him! I blushed at the thought, silenced by shame.

"I will not let him harm you," Bathory vowed heatedly.

"I believe you," I replied. "Your nearness drives the darkness away."

So here I am, writing in a different bed, in a different room. It is more modest, but I prefer it, being closer to Bathory.

What hold does Quincey have over me? Why am I so unable to resist him? Even when he spares me his supernatural powers of seduction, he overcomes me and awakes in me an unholy desire. Thank God, I have Bathory to keep my senses well grounded, to make me feel safe.

4TH DECEMBER 1918

Lord Bathory shook me gently awake before dawn.

Having not long been asleep, I struggled into consciousness. "What is it?" I asked drowsily.

"I am sorry to wake you," he apologized, leaning over me. "But there is something you should see."

Confused, I sat up and smoothed my hair. "What is it?" I asked.

"It is something that will let you rest easy from this day on," Bathory told me seriously.

I pulled my dressing gown from where it lay at the foot of my bed. "Do tell me what it is," I begged, wrapping the robe around me and rising.

"You shall see soon enough," Bathory promised.

He led me down to the kitchens and past a huge wooden table stacked with dishes and pans.

"Where are we going?" I asked him breathlessly.

"To the cellars," he told me. He led me by the hand down more stairs, our footsteps echoing eerily—and then on again, down a narrow twisting staircase that descended into a dim basement. The air smelled dank, and its coldness pierced my robe. I shivered.

"Please, Xavier—tell me what we are going to see," I begged. My voice echoed from the walls, and even I heard the anxiety in it.

"Not long to wait now, Mary!" Bathory said. "We are nearly there. I don't want to spoil the surprise. . . ."

A small corridor lay at the base of the stairs. Shelves ran the length of it, each one packed tight with jars and tins and bottles. I glanced around in bewilderment. What sort of prize could lie in such a place? Then I saw a door ahead, wooden except for a small round window in its center.

"The cold room," Bathory announced, drawing me toward it. "It is where we store our meat."

"Your meat?" I asked uncertainly. Had he awoken me to show me what we would have at dinner that evening?

Bathory flicked a switch to the side of the door. A weak electric bulb lit the room with a gloomy yellowish glow. "Look through the window." He smiled.

I peered anxiously through, my heart pounding with unease. I had never before known Bathory to behave so capriciously. He had never shown the slightest penchant for mystery. "I see nothing but meat, hanging," I murmured. And then a movement on the floor caught my eye. It was a figure, struggling to sit up. Through the blood and bruises that marked it, I recognized Quincey's face.

Shock and pain skewered my heart, and I stepped hastily backward. "You caught him!" I breathed.

I struggled against the compassion that cried within me. Quincey looked so defeated, so battered. What had Bathory done to him?

"Do not worry, he is safely locked in!" Bathory pointed to a heavy bolt near the base of the door. "You are safe now from his evil scheming."

So. Quincey is trapped at last. I should be pleased, shouldn't I? So why does my heart feel as bruised as his poor face?

CHAPTER 22

*Journal of
Mary Seward*

5TH DECEMBER 1918

Lily haunted my dreams once more. I awoke—or thought I
awoke—and saw her, luminescent in the shadowy darkness
of my room. She beckoned me from my bed with a twisted
and bloody hand. Her eyes glittered anxiously, and she fluttered at my bedside as though agitated.

"Lily, why do you wake me again?" I asked. "All is safe
now. There is no need to fear."

She did not seem to hear me. A frantic look of anguish
possessed her disfigured face, and she urged me to rise with
an ever more urgently waving hand.

"What is it, Lily?" I asked her, longing for her to speak.
But she said nothing, only began to cry. Blood-tinged tears
soaked her bruised and broken cheek. Then she beckoned
again and glided out into the hallway.

I could not deny the desperation in her gaze. I grabbed
my robe and chased after her along the corridors we had
traced before.

The rugs felt silky beneath my feet, and the cold air carried the smoky fragrance of dying embers. My heart pounded
ever harder in my chest, for I knew where Lily was leading
me—to the same part of the house she had brought me to
before. Reluctantly I forced myself to follow until I recognized the dreaded door. It stood before me—closed this
time—looming like a headstone. Fear pierced me like an icy
wind and froze the blood inside my veins. Last time I had
found John inside this room. Would I again have to endure
his hideous presence? I could not bear it. But Lily pointed
toward the door and beseeched me with her eyes. I knew I
must open it.

I steeled myself and placed my hand on the handle. It felt
oddly warm beneath my fingers, as though a fire burned
within. I turned it, trembling, and pushed wide the door.

Joyous relief bathed me like a cool breeze as I was met
not with a feeding, vampiric John, but a sleeping Bathory,
breathing peacefully as a child. His face was turned from me,
and I lingered on the threshold, wanting to snatch a glimpse
of him in repose.

With a smile, I tiptoed in, looking curiously around me as
I went. I stopped short when I noticed something at the foot
of the bed. The milk white body of a woman became visible,

lying on the rug. She was naked, and her head was twisted, her broken neck showing the red stain where she had been bitten.

What was this? My head swam in confusion. Vomit rose in my throat, and I swallowed hard against it. Before I could move, Bathory rolled his head in sleep and turned his face toward me. A dribble of blood oozed from lips that parted slightly to reveal a single, gleaming white fang.

No. No, this wasn't possible! I covered my mouth with both hands, pressing back the scream of terror and disbelief that struggled to burst forth. And then I realized that some-one was lying next to Bathory—a woman, clothed in rich green satin that camouflaged her against the green quilt. As I stared, I realized that there was something strangely familiar about her—her jawline, her mouth, her nose, her brow. . . . I searched my memory to place her—this woman, sleeping so peacefully beside the man who swore he loved me.

I gasped in shock as the answer came to me. Without the glasses and the fiercely scraped-back hair . . . there was no mistaking her—

Becky Morrow.

I turned to find Lily, to demand why she had conjured such a dream for me—but Lily had gone. I felt a chill draft blow into the room, bringing goose bumps to my flesh. And in that moment of physical sensation, I understood.

This was no dream. I was not asleep.

This was real.

Lily had come—a spirit in the mortal world—to warn me of the deception.

I stood there I'm not certain how long, struggling to come to terms with what I had learned—staring again at Bathory, who now seemed a complete stranger to me.

And Becky—dear, kind Becky, who had nursed Father and been such company for me in my grief? How did *she* come to be here? Was she a victim as Lily had been? Had she been seduced by the vampire who now lay before me?

Quincey's warning rang in my ears. *Bathory is dangerous!* He *had* been trying to save me.

Trembling from head to toe, I backed away toward the door.

If this is no dream, I told myself, I can at least attempt to control what happens next. I turned and fled down the corridor. I had to free Quincey. If we were facing a vampire, another vampire might be our only hope.

I must release him, I told myself—the idea hammering in my head to the rhythm of my pounding feet. I ran and ran, turning through this corridor and that until at last I found the head of the stairs. I raced down them two at a time and sped across the entrance hall and down through the servants' passage.

My bare feet made hardly any sound as I raced through the kitchens. I caught a glimpse out of one of the windows.

The sun was red and low in the sky. I had slept nearly the whole day!

I had to hurry. Bathory would soon be waking.

As I passed the table, my fingers brushed a handle and sent a teetering pile of pans clattering to the floor. The noise rang from the white-washed walls and echoed through the halls. But I did not pause. I thought only of reaching Quincey. Nothing must prevent me.

I half slid down the ill-lit cellar stairs. The door was ahead of me. I rushed to it and, grasping the heavy bolt, drew it back with a dull clank.

The door swung open, and I saw Quincey's eyes gleaming like a wolf's in the shadows. "Quincey," I panted. "I have seen Bathory. I know what he is!"

Quincey slowly drew himself to his feet.

"You must help me!" I begged. "I cannot escape here alone!"

"I no longer have the strength I once had," Quincey rasped. "Bathory is more powerful than I . . . now."

I looked at him for a moment, and I knew that the world was not so black and white as once I had imagined. I drew back my sleeve to reveal my freckled forearm. "Here!" I cried. "Take some of my blood. It will give you the strength you need for us both to escape."

"No, Mary." Quincey shook his head. "I will not taint you. But I will do what I can." He moved from his cold prison, mounting the twisting stairs two at a time. I marveled that there was still strength enough left in him and raced after. I could hear his breathing, hard and labored, but still he raced on, holding his hand out behind him so that I might grab it. Together we dashed through the kitchen. The sun had sunk below the horizon now. We made our way up into the entrance hall.

A great pool of moonlight flooded from the windows. I prayed Bathory had not yet awoken, but as we crossed the polished stone floor, a shadow fell across it. Bathory emerged to bar our path, smiling triumphantly.

My stomach tightened with rage and terror. I heard footsteps on the stairs behind us and turned. Becky descended the stairs slowly, regal as a princess in her green gown. She smiled broadly, revealing her pristine white fangs—her gaze locked on Quincey.

Confusion gripped me. She seemed no victim now. Indeed, she was more beautiful than I could ever have imagined, her chin proudly tilted and her auburn hair cascading around her oval face.

I saw now. She had taken great pains to hide her beauty, for it would have marked her out above any woman.

"Late as ever, Rebecca," Bathory chided, and, like a falconer receiving his hawk, he held out his hand to her as she glided to his side.

She turned and addressed him fondly. "A lady's prerogative . . ." Her Irish brogue had disappeared, replaced now by an imperious clipped tone that sounded nothing like that of the unassuming girl I had known at the sanatorium.

Dear God, Becky was no victim at all! She was a vampire like Bathory.

With a sickening jolt, I realized that I had invited her into my home to play companion to my father! And her work at the sanatorium. Could it have been Becky feeding off the patients all along?

"You—you killed my father!" I shrieked at her.

Becky gave me a dismissive smile. "Oh yes, your father . . . He really was very sweet," she purred. "But sadly, I didn't have the pleasure of killing him. He was trying to escape me when he met with his accident."

I longed to fly at her and scratch out her eyes, but Quincey grasped my hand and held me back.

"And before you ask—those soldiers at the ward?" Becky went on, her eyes glowing seductively. "I assure you, they were grateful for my attentions after I'd persuaded them. . . ."

"Well, you shall not persuade us!" I shouted.

"Really?" Bathory's gray eyes were now cold as slate, devoid of all feeling for me. The gentle gaze I'd come to trust had gone forever. Without warning, he stepped forward and thrust his fist at Quincey's chest, sending him flying backward as though tossed by a giant.

I gasped, never imagining such superhuman strength lay concealed in Bathory's slim physique.

Quincey rolled as he crashed to the floor and staggered at once to his feet, breathing heavily.

Becky glared at Bathory, anger lighting her eyes. "Be careful with him! He is not as strong as once he was," she told him.

I stared at Quincey. "Have you met her before?" I demanded.

"Yes," Quincey replied between gasps. "That is Lady Rebecca Bathory, Lord Bathory's sister."

"Bathory's sister?" I whispered.

Quincey nodded. "She is renowned among our kind," he added curtly, "as a skilled seductress."

I saw that his eyes burned with a reproach that hinted at intimacy. With a sting of jealousy, I realized that Quincey spoke with the voice of experience.

"I am flattered, Quincey," Becky murmured alluringly. "I have thought of you often these many years. It was my hope that someday our destinies would intertwine and that we could be again what we once were."

"We were nothing," he snarled. "Do not pretend otherwise."

Becky's eyes flashed. "You worshiped me once! And now we can resume our affair. Once *she* is out of the way." She shot me a look of pure disdain.

Bathory stepped forward then, his gaze now burning with a fiery menace. He snarled, his curled lip revealing his glistening fangs. "To hell with your girlish infatuation, Rebecca!

We have a task to finish." He turned toward Quincey. "I suppose it would be wise to deal with you first."

My heart seemed to freeze in my chest. Quincey was now so weak and Bathory so strong! Quincey could never win such a fight.

I reached for the vial of holy water at my throat. But as I fumbled beneath the collar of my nightgown, a hideous realization gripped me.

It was gone!

"Looking for this?" Bathory took something from his pocket and dangled it before him. My chain, with the vial swinging from it!

As I clasped my throat, vulnerable now, my horror mounted. "How did you . . . ?" I croaked.

"I took it while you were sleeping, of course," he answered smoothly. He slipped the vial back into his pocket. "Poor, powerless Mary. Now you must simply watch—and wait your turn." He turned to Quincey and lifted his fist.

"Leave him, brother!" Rebecca shouted.

Bathory hesitated a moment. It was the moment Quincey needed. Before Bathory could land a blow, Quincey raised an arm and deflected his aim. With his other hand, he punched Bathory hard on the jaw.

Bathory collapsed to the ground and spat a puddle of black, oily blood onto the marble floor. As Quincey stared down at him, panting from his effort, Bathory flexed his

shoulders and gave a roar so filled with fury that it fixed terror in my heart. If Bathory got to his feet, Quincey would
never manage to defeat such rage. I had to do something.

Glancing quickly around the walls, I saw, resting on
brackets, an ancient war ax, with two curving blades that
gleamed in the moonlight. I ran to it and dragged it down. Its
over-mighty head swung toward the floor, and I struggled to
control it. But my arms were infused with desperation, and
somehow I found the strength to heave its blades back into
the air.

Becky stared at me, her eyes burning with fire. She hissed
and drew back her lips to reveal her deadly fangs.

I stormed toward Bathory. He was still on his knees, wip-
ing the blood from his lips, but his sister's hiss alerted him
and he looked quickly up at Quincey, expecting another
blow.

Catching him unawares, I swung the ax.

It sliced his head clean from his shoulders. The beats of
his ruined heart sent a fountain of blood spurting from his
neck and his head. His body fell to the ground with a dull
crack, and his head rolled over so that his face stared up at
the vaulted ceiling, his eyes still wide with shock as the fire
in them faded.

Perspiration prickled on my brow, and I let the heavy head
of the ax rest on the ground, though I would not let go of the
handle. I crouched and fumbled in Bathory's jacket pocket,

swallowing hard against the bile that rose in my throat. I had to get my vial back. I felt its delicate chain and grasped it, drawing it out and clasping it thankfully in my hand.

Becky had staggered back, bent double as though punched in the stomach. She pressed her hand over her mouth, horrified. A wrenching sob exploded from her.

Then she turned her stricken gaze on Quincey. "Surely you won't kill me as well?" she whispered. "After what we shared?"

Quincey shook his head wearily. "I loved you once, Rebecca. But your cruelty to Mary I cannot forgive."

Becky stared in disbelief. "You sound as if you love her!"

"With all my soul," he answered without hesitation.

My heart soared even as Becky's stare hardened into pure malice. She glanced at Bathory's corpse. "Then I am glad that we agreed to do as we were bid!" she hissed. "*He* told us that Mary should be tormented before she died. *He* said a quick death was not enough; that she deserved something crueler—and now I agree!"

"He?" Quincey asked coldly.

I found myself struggling to understand what Becky meant. Who could she mean?

Rebecca gazed at Quincey, a triumphant smile spreading across her face.

"Who? Who is it that ordered you to torture Mary?" Quincey demanded.

I heard movement behind us and turned to peer into the shadows—expecting to find a servant staring fearfully at the bloody scene before us. But I could see no one.

"It was I," answered a deep voice. And then a cloaked figure stepped into the moonlight.

It was no servant who had spoken.

It was my former fiancé, John Shaw.

CHAPTER 23

*Journal of
Mary Seward*

5TH *DECEMBER 1918 (CONTINUED)*

He was more powerful and muscular than I remembered him. His face had grown hard and weathered. I hardly recognized the pale young soldier who had returned trembling from the trenches two years ago. How savage his gaze had become. And though I now knew his heritage, the blood in my veins turned to ice when he smiled to reveal his strong vampire fangs.

I grew numb with fear as John slowly approached us. I hardly felt the ax as it slipped from my grip and instinctively backed toward Quincey, pressing my body against his. If we were to die, then at least we would die together.

Rebecca watched John as a dog watches its master, nervous of his every move.

He nodded at her, his eyes betraying no warmth. "You've done well," he congratulated her. "As did your brother—until he underestimated Mary. I did warn you both she would not be easy prey." His gaze fell on me, and a malicious smile touched his lips. "Mary, it has been a pleasure to torment you."

"I should never have believed that such darkness lay within you," I whispered.

"It has not all come from within," John answered smoothly. "Some has been nurtured by circumstance and some by sheer hard work." He smoothed his pale hair with his hand. "What do you think I've been doing these past two years?"

"I do not wish to know!" I turned my face from him.

"You do not care that I was left alone in that grim castle?" he asked acidly. "No, of course not. You ran from me. Left me there to live out my cursed fate. But you'll be pleased to know I spent my time there wisely, learning all I could, gaining strength and knowledge. And, of course, hatching this little scheme to entrap you and Quincey. It was in Father's papers that I discovered the close bonds of loyalty between the Bathory and the Tepes family. It seemed natural to exploit such a union."

He glanced at Quincey for the first time. "It was most vindicating, how keen Rebecca was to help me punish you for your disloyalty, Quincey."

Rebecca's eyes searched Quincey's. "No. That's not true. We were only supposed to return you to the fold—"

John laughed, a harsh shout devoid of warmth. "Don't be

absurd. Perhaps you have forgotten, my dear, what you called him. What was it? An ungrateful fool?"

His scorching gaze swept back to Quincey and then to me. "Now look at you both! My dear brother and my fiancée, huddling together like a pair of trembling lovers!"

"I am no longer your fiancée!" I cried.

"I am crushed," he sneered sarcastically. "Although . . . how ironic that you should reject me because of what I have become—and yet now fawn over Quincey, who is guilty of the same crimes."

"He is trying to turn his back on his dark nature," I retorted. "You started with every advantage and yet when offered a chance for evil, you took it wholeheartedly!"

My words seemed to anger him, for the smile evaporated from his face and his eyes burned hotter. "I had every advantage?" he roared. "I had nothing. It was he who had every advantage—the loving family, the knowledge of who he was—and he rejected it all. Betrayed all who had loved and nurtured him."

Why did Quincey not defend himself? I turned to look up into his handsome, troubled face. He was staring at John, his eyes unfathomable. But his body was still pressed against mine, drained to the point of collapse by the weakness that afflicted him.

John stepped forward toward Quincey. "I am the stronger now," he gloated. "I'm sorry you have made it easy for me to

destroy you by weakening yourself these past two years.
Nevertheless"—he rubbed his hands together slowly and plucked a medieval sword from the wall—"I think I shall still enjoy this."

Quincey growled a warning, but I heard the weakness in him and so did John, for his eyes lighted with triumph. He swung back his sword and flexed his arm, preparing for the first strike.

Quincey lifted his hands to defend himself as John let out a terrifying roar and unleashed a powerful blow.

"No!" a voice cried out.

In a flash of green, I saw Rebecca fling herself in front of Quincey. She gave a piercing scream of agony as John's vicious blade sliced through her body. John stared in surprise at her as she crashed onto the hard marble floor. In that instant, I saw my chance. I uncorked the vial still clasped in my hand. Leaping forward, I flung the entire contents into John's face.

The holy water splashed his right eye, and smoke steamed as the flesh burnt and bubbled beneath it. John screamed in agony and tore at the smoldering flesh as the water soaked deeper in, burning through to bone. He tore from the entrance hall, his cries echoing in the empty house.

I turned back to see Quincey kneeling beside Rebecca's broken body and hurried over to them.

"I did not know he planned to kill you . . ." Rebecca gasped as Quincey gently raised her head. "I thought he meant only to bring you back to your bloodline." Her eyes flickered with red and then softened into tenderness. A black stain spread across her gown where she had been sliced through.

Rebecca clutched Quincey's hand. "I've loved you, Quincey, ever since I was sent to seduce you," she confessed. "Will there never again be a place for me in your heart?"

Quincey hesitated. "You were my first love, Rebecca, and for that you will always hold a place in my heart."

Rebecca drew in a shuddering breath and nodded.

"He will kill you as soon as he is able," Quincey said.

Rebecca closed her eyes and nodded. "I know, and it is right. Leave me now to await my fate."

Quincey laid her head softly on the floor, and I could not tell if there was regret in his dark gaze as he gave Rebecca one final look.

He said nothing more to her as he straightened and drew me to my feet. "We must escape while John is wounded," he said.

Pulling my hand, he led me to the door, and together we ran out onto the wide driveway. The cold night air froze me to the bone. Quincey quickly slipped off his greatcoat and put it around me. As he buttoned it hurriedly, I heard an almighty roar. My heart lurched in terror, and I looked back up at the house. Silhouetted in the doorway stood John. I could see the burnt-out hole where his eye had been.

I stifled a horrified sob. How could we escape? Nothing surrounded us but the empty moor. We were trapped in this dreadful place.

"I think I can carry us away from here," Quincey rasped. He took my hands, and squeezing them between his, he stared into my eyes. "Do not be afraid," he urged. "I will fly us to Father Michael. He may give us sanctuary. Even if he turns me away, he will take you in."

I trembled at his words. What did he mean to do? He let go of my hands and stepped away. "Close your eyes, Mary," he commanded. "And don't open them again until I tell you to."

I did as he bid and heard him utter a groan, deep and guttural. A few moments later, I felt the night air stir around me and heard the eerie swishing noise of huge wings.

Keeping my eyes tightly closed, I felt long, hard talons curve around my shoulders and my waist. And then I felt the ground fall away beneath my feet. I clung to Quincey as he transported us across the night sky.

Sometime later, though my eyes were still closed, I sensed a glimmer of light on the horizon. Dawn was coming. I felt Quincey dip—and feared that the first rays of sun had injured him. I almost opened my eyes in panic but then felt a sudden *whump* and realized that Quincey had landed. He laid me gently on the ground and moved away from me. I could feel the pricking of heather upon my face.

Feeling a little dizzy with relief, I slowly struggled to my feet and dared to open my eyes. I saw the outskirts of a city before us—Exeter was just ahead.

"I could not make it," Quincey gasped.

I turned in time to see him shimmer back into human form. "We are far enough away to be safe," I reassured him.

He nodded but then began to stagger. I hurried over to him, grasping his arms to steady him. He felt heavy against me. "The sunlight is fatal to me," he breathed.

On the horizon, the pale blue glow of morning threatened to burst into golden rays. I scanned the empty edge of heath where we had landed, looking desperately for shelter.

"We are near the catacombs," he gasped.

"Which way?" I demanded.

He pointed to a rocky outcrop a hundred yards away. "An entrance is there," he murmured.

I strode toward it, dragging Quincey with me. He staggered at my side, and I struggled under the weight of him. But I would not let him fall. All the while the horizon lightened, and panic began to grip me. I could not let the sun destroy him after all we had been through. Ignoring my hammering heart, I half dragged, half carried him toward the shadowy entrance that loomed now before us.

At last we collapsed within its quiet shadows and I lay panting on the floor beside him. Such silence and stillness. I could hear water dripping farther back in the cave and wondered how far it led into the depths of the earth.

I rolled onto my side and leaned toward Quincey. His breathing was shallow and strained. Alarm twisted my heart. "Quincey!" I put my hand on his ice-cold cheek.

He opened his eyes, and the early morning light that seeped now into the cave made them shine like onyx as he turned his head and gazed at me lying beside him. "Dear Mary," he breathed weakly. "How I wish I could have defeated the vampire part of my nature and lived on."

"You speak as though you are going to die!" My voice was sharp as anger flared in me. I could not lose him now!

"You are all I shall miss," he went on. "My heart beats only for you. But you must go. Seek sanctuary. You have defeated us twice, and I am glad of it."

"No!" I cried. "Take some of my blood. Please. If that is what you need to survive, you may have it." Before he could argue, I dragged my wrist over the sharp stones of the cave floor, tearing the flesh until blood flowed. There was less pain in my arm than howled in my heart. I held my wrist above his lips and let the blood drip from my wounds into his mouth. His eyes flared as the liquid bathed his tongue, and he groaned. He lifted his hands and pressed my wrist harder to his face.

I felt the sharp points of his fangs. How I longed for him to sink them in! But he only ran his tongue over my skin and licked clean the blood before releasing me.

"Please go," he murmured, closing his eyes.

"I cannot leave you." Tears choked my voice, and I held back a sob.

"Go!" he commanded.

I stumbled to my feet, a pain in my chest crueler than any I had known before.

The entrance of the cave was lit by a rosy dawn and I walked toward it, my feet unsteady on the rocky ground. I did not glance back to see him lying there. I did not want my last memory of him to be of one defeated. Instead I walked out into the light and felt its meager warmth upon my face.

CHAPTER 24

Journal of Mary Seward

Purfleet seemed no different when I arrived back here almost four weeks ago. Dust had hardly gathered on the furniture at home. But I felt utterly changed. No more would the world be ruled for me by the rigorous routine of day and night; instead it would always seem a dappled place where darkness and light played together as shadows beneath a tree.

When I pushed open the front door, the top letter among the others on the mat was from Dr. McLeod. It told me simply that my name had been cleared at the sanatorium and asked me to visit him.

I went, of course. What else was there for me to do? I hoped I might obtain my former employment there. A hollowness had opened in my chest since leaving Quincey, a space I knew I must fill with some distraction if I were not to slip into despair.

And so I put on my coat this afternoon, walked the familiar route to the hospital, and asked at the reception desk for Dr. McLeod. As Flora plugged her telephone into the switchboard and called his office, she looked at me curiously.

"A man was looking for you before Christmas," she told me. "Dark, handsome fellow, he was."

Quincey?

Flora held up a hand and spoke into her mouthpiece. "Mary Seward is here for Dr. McLeod," she said. There was a moment of silence during which she nodded. "Very well," she finished. "Goodbye."

She unplugged her headset and turned back to me. "You're to go right up, and quickly. Dr. McLeod is scheduled to operate in half an hour."

"Thank you." I hurried away from her desk and climbed the stairs that I knew led to his office. I knocked upon the frosted glass of his door and heard his familiar voice from within.

"Come in."

I entered the room and took the chair he offered me. As I smoothed my skirt over my knees, he sat down behind his cluttered desk and folded his hands beneath his chin.

"It seems I owe you an apology, Miss Seward," he began. His eyes had a dark and worried look.

"What else could you have presumed when you caught me?" I conceded. I kept my voice steady, though my heart remembered with a jolt that grisly dusk when I had staked Sergeant Hopkins.

"We are still not sure what happened," Dr. McLeod admitted. "But we are certain you were not the cause. Though you clearly knew more than you would admit."

I leaned forward in my chair, feeling for the first time un-intimidated by the doctor's status and bearing. In this field, I was the expert and he the student. "And what should I have told you? That some unnatural fiend was loose in the hospital?"

Dr. McLeod looked at me uncertainly, sweat breaking out on his brow. "It has certainly been a strange affair," he admitted. "And I could not have believed it if it had not been witnessed by Sister herself."

"What happened to convince you of my innocence?" I asked him. The thought had often crossed my mind since I'd received his letter.

"Another nurse was caught red-handed stealing blood from one of the patients," Dr. McLeod stated. He was trying to appear detached, but he tapped his pen anxiously on his notepad as he spoke.

"Stealing?" I queried.

"Drinking," he admitted. His face paled at the thought. "Lieutenant Moreau. The night sister caught her in the act."

"And which nurse was it?" I knew the answer but still wanted to hear Dr. McLeod's confirmation.

"Becky Morrow," he muttered.

"What did she do when she was caught?" I asked. I knew now what "modest" Becky was capable of.

"She just laughed." Dr. McLeod drew a handkerchief from his pocket and wiped his brow. "And then she twisted Lieutenant Moreau's neck until it snapped."

He closed his eyes momentarily as though grappling anew with the shock.

"Was the night sister all right?" I demanded.

"Well, she was shocked, of course, and called for help, but when the other nurses came and saw Nurse Morrow, her face smeared with blood, they just stood and stared in shock. Morrow simply walked past them all and out of the hospital. By the time we had alerted the police, she had disappeared."

Dr. McLeod put away his handkerchief and leaned upon his desk. "Miss Seward. Mary . . ." he began falteringly. "I believe we were most cruelly duped by this fiend, and we owe you an apology for ever laying the blame at your door. I hope you can forgive and return to us."

I stared at him, hope springing like a bird in my chest. "You would really take me?" I asked.

"There are still wounded soldiers to be cared for, though not so many now that hostilities are over," Dr. McLeod replied gravely. "We would welcome your experience to finish things up here. . . ."

"You are most kind," I thanked him. "Yes. I would like to return to my duties at the hospital."

The doctor's face broke into a relieved smile

"But," I went on. There was one proviso I would need to add. "I will still only work during daylight hours."

Dr. McLeod nodded.

We agreed that I would start as soon as the new year began—and then I left.

Since then, I have hardly left the house. I had hidden away over Christmas, my heart absorbed in its own grief. But today, I visited the Edwardses. I'd felt a strong need to see Grace.

Jane answered the door. I saw that the hall behind her was still festooned with green garlands and scarlet bows. Her face broke into a smile upon her seeing me. "There were rumors you had returned!" She leaned forward and kissed me on the cheek. "I knew you would call as soon as you felt able."

She drew me into the house and relieved me of my coat and bonnet. "Grace is with Andrew in the parlor," she said, beckoning me toward the parlor door.

I gazed at her gratefully. She'd made no comment about my departure or my pale and lackluster appearance, and I knew it was kindness rather than lack of consideration that moved her.

"We've had a most delightful Christmas," she told me as she showed me in. "Grace's face simply glows with happiness every time we light the candles on the tree." She pressed a buzzer in the wall. "I'll ring for the maid. We can all have some tea."

Andrew stood to greet me, laughing as Grace rushed over to me, clapping her chubby hands. "Nice to see you again, Mary," he said. "We missed you over Christmas. Where on earth were you?"

"I'm sure Mary will tell us all about her adventures when she's ready." Jane flashed Andrew a warning glance.

"Oh, there's little to tell." I swung Grace up into my arms and held her close. "Grief over Father has made me reclusive."

"There, Andrew," Jane said warmly. "Just as I thought." She touched my arm. "We're glad to have you back with us in time for New Year's. Indeed, we have planned a party for tonight—just a small gathering. Would you like to come?"

Unease pricked in my palms. The memory of meeting Lord Bathory at Jane's last soiree was still fresh. And as long as John was still alive and bent on revenge, it would be unwise to be out at night. Who knew what he would plan next? "I am a little tired," I told her. "Perhaps another time."

"Very well," Jane agreed easily. "Do sit down."

I took a chair beside the hearth and Grace settled on my knee. I kissed her fondly on the nose. As I did so, she laughed the pure, spontaneous laugh of a young child. In that perfect moment, peace swept through me. Even though horror had returned to haunt me, Father's words echoed in my heart.

"Knowing there is darkness should not stop us from reveling in the light."

I played with Grace until the maid brought the tea and then sipped it quickly so I might leave before dusk began to fall.

The sun was setting by the time I reached home. I locked the door securely behind me and ran my fingers over the crucifix in the hall. How Rebecca must have hated passing it each day.

I drew the curtains to keep out the dark and hold in the warmth. As I pulled the drapes together, feeling the heavy fabric brush against my skin, I heard a noise, the tap of nails upon the glass.

My heart leapt, torn between hope and horror. Was it John? Quincey? Either way, I had to look.

I peered around the curtain and saw eyes, familiar, glowing through the glass.

Quincey!

I raced to the front door and threw it open. "Come in . . ." I breathed.

He stepped across the threshold, and I saw at once that he had recovered his old strength. And beauty. He towered above me, his head held high, his cheeks no longer gaunt, his hair slicked back and shining in the hall light.

I embraced him at once. "Oh, Quincey, how I have missed you!" I sighed. I felt his arms slide round me. His heart beat fiercely beneath my cheek.

"And I you," he murmured. His breath ruffled my hair, and that gentle sensation was enough to set my body tingling with desire.

But I knew why he had come—why he looked so reinvigorated. He was here to confess, and I did not want to hear it. I did not want to know that once more, he was following his vampire nature and feeding on human blood.

"Mary . . ." he began.

Desperately I pressed my fingers over his lips. "Do not say it," I begged, gazing into the dark depths of his eyes.

He gently drew my hand aside. "You know I cannot allow myself to be weak any longer," he insisted. "John will come again. I must be ready for it, for if he harmed you, I could not bear it." He looked at me, his loving gaze tinged with anxiety.

Resigned, I dropped my gaze and rested my cheek against his powerful chest once more. "I know." I sighed again. "I wish it were not so, but I understand."

I do not know which hurt me more—that Quincey had let the dark side of his soul return to dominance to protect me— or that in his doing so, I was not able to be with him.

How I hated John for forcing this upon us. "I pray he comes soon," I whispered bitterly. "Then we can deal with him once and for all!"

Quincey lifted my chin and gazed at me, his eyes brimming with sorrow. He leaned down and brushed my lips with the gentlest of kisses. I understood why he did not risk more, for I knew well the passion that flared so easily between us and where it might lead.

"I will never be far," he told me. Then he took his leave.

Even now as I write, I feel a strange awareness of him. His presence will touch me so long as he is on this earth. The yearning in my heart will never cease. He has captured my heart and my soul, and I am his until I die.

Sleep well, dear Quincey, wherever you are, and dream of me as I shall dream of you.

Journal of
Quincey Harker

31ST DECEMBER 1918

I am safe in the shadows now. It is cold here, but it will always be cold wherever Mary is not.

To have been so close to her tonight was almost more than I could bear, knowing I would leave her with only one chaste kiss. But if I am to safeguard her, it must be this way.

I will love her and love her and love her from afar. And from this place, I shall watch over her and do all in my power to protect her.

No matter what evil may plague us next.